PSIONIC ECHO

THE DEVIL IS IN THE DETAILS

THE PSIONIC SEQUENCE BOOK TWO

PSIONIC ECHO

THE DEVIL IS IN THE DETAILS

MICHAEL DAVID

ROGUE
RIVER

An Imprint of Roan & Weatherford Publishing Associates, LLC
Bentonville, Arkansas
www.roanweatherford.com

Copyright © 2024 by Michael David

Library of Congress Cataloging-in-Publication Data
Names: David, Michael author.
Title: Psionic Echo/Michael David | The Psionic Sequence #2
Description: First Edition. | Bentonville: Rogue River, 2024.
Identifiers: LCCN: 2024934918 | ISBN: 978-1-63373-911-6 (trade paperback) |
ISBN: 978-1-63373-912-3 (eBook)
Subjects: | BISAC: FICTION/Thrillers/Supernatural |
FICTION/Thrillers/Psychological | FICTION/Thrillers/Suspense
LC record available at: https://lccn.loc.gov/2024934918

Rogue River trade paperback edition May, 2024

Cover & Interior Design by Casey W. Cowan
Editing by George "Clay" Mitchell & Amy Cowan

*This book is dedicated to the memory of Janet Edwards.
I miss making you laugh and your awesome sense of humor.
When I scared the bejesus out of you, you never got mad
because you appreciated a good joke, even if it was on you!*

I WANT TO ACKNOWLEDGE THE invaluable help of my critique group buddies. Sincere thanks to Jodi, Linda, and Taylor. You're the best! Thanks also to Casey Cowan for overseeing The Psionic Sequence series and my editor, George "Clay" Mitchell. I couldn't have done this without you guys!

1

THE DOMINANT
CONSCIOUSNESS

A TEXAS SUMMER BREEZE STIRS my hair as I finish my iced tea under the shade of the roofed patio. In a perfect world, I never would have killed my parents. But this isn't a perfect world, and I did. I emptied a syringe—a syringe of medicine into their veins to wake them from a dimensional induction trance.

The U.S. government had employed my parents in a psychic espionage program that eventually went bad. Allen Costas, the program director, wanted Mom and Dad to spy on the U.S. for his financial gain, instead of focusing on foreign enemy intelligence. When my parents refused to sell out their country, Costas kidnapped me, Archer Ann Wilson, and threatened my life.

As an adept psychic, I stayed one step ahead of the director, until it came time to administer an intravenous drug to awaken my parents from their dimensional trance. But, Costas had his henchman, Le Cadavre, switch the wake-up dose for a fatal overdose—guaranteeing death by my hand. Unable to help either parent, I watched them suffer and die—violently, painfully—while Le Cadavre smirked.

Even though both parents were dead and my boyfriend, Slash, indirectly murdered by Costas, I had the next best thing.

In a perfect world, I never would have killed my parents. But, in an alternate dimension, much like the planet Earth, it doesn't matter. Because of the dimensional induction drug developed by Costas's scientists, I had achieved unification with my dead loved ones. My astral spirit had journeyed to a parallel world where my alternate family and Slash were alive and willing to accept me as I was—the dominant consciousness within their own daughter's mind. I had dubbed her, Archer 1, and we both shared the same body, the same passions, and the same psychic abilities. Except for two differences, and they're a heart stopper, I have the power to halt time and can kill with my mind.

The afternoon sun brings the outdoor temperature up to ninety degrees, and the sizzle and smell as Father grills steaks, awakens my hunger. Slash, my bad boy lover approaches and shoves his honey-blond hair from his eyes. The outer corner of his lip lifts in his trademark sneer, and a new lip labret sparkles in the sun. But he is on a mission and moves closer, puts his cheek against mine, and poses for a selfie.

I pucker up and give him a wet one. Slash is pleased but tries to look annoyed. We both grin like fools as he snaps our picture. Crazy in love will do that to you.

Mother approaches with a fresh glass of iced tea and looks down as I glance up. Even in an alternate world, it's like facing a mirror. We're both tall for our gender, with the same brown hair and porcelain blue eyes. But I'm impressed with the deep compassion and intelligence that fits comfortably on Mother's face, a graceful lesson from thirty-nine years of life.

She places her hand on my stomach. "I've planned a baby shower for you right after the wedding."

That will be six months to the day past my twenty-first birthday, and I can't wait.

I take a sip of tea and sigh. The world I left is eerily similar to this one. The parents' houses are the same, and everyone looks alike, but the sky in this alternate planet is pale yellow. Tara the Traveler, who monitors journeyers between alternate worlds and acts as Time Guardian, had warned me that some things could be a bit off. So far, I am pleased with my new life and welcome its normalcy. With a wedding not too far away and a baby boy due shortly after that, well, it just adds to the stability I crave and justly deserve.

Slash wanders over to help my father load up the steaks when something moves. A dark vibration runs through the fabric of my new home. Something not normal. Something not good.

I look for recognition upon the men's faces. Find nothing, until I glance at my tea. A concentric ripple starts from the outer edge of the liquid and moves inward. Not once, not twice, but three times.

My scalp prickles.

My psychic sense tingles.

My breath bucks up my throat.

I rise quickly. "Mom, Dad, Slash, hold that steak for me. I'll be back in a minute." Streaking through the kitchen and into the living room, I stand in front of the pivoting bookcase, then visualize the doorway at the heart of time.

2

THE FOUR ELEMENTS

I REPEAT, "TIME, TIME, TIME," and find myself in the Time Guardian's apartment. This room is the entry point for all dimensional travelers, and when I'm not residing with my family, I act as the official guide and assistant Guardian. A few quick steps across the living room, and I open the door to the Hallway of Infinity. Beige doors, spaced evenly every seven feet on either side, extend forever. Having been here before, I know each one opens upon an alternate reality—parallel worlds similar to the one I just left.

Similar but not exactly alike. I think of the baby boy in my womb and know an Alternate Archer in a parallel existence might carry a girl instead. Or no child at all. For better or worse, the paths we don't take in this life play out with our doppelgangers in other worlds.

The hallway floor vibrates from a hidden source, and I move to the door on my left. I grasp the knob and open it wide, just as the Statue of Liberty topples. The three-hundred-foot tall monument tilts to the left and falls as the earth beneath breaks open and fills with water. I bring my hands to my face and watch as the landmark slides into the churning sea, followed by a great plume of water that gushes around the green, oxidized structure. Ellis Island groans and moves and rips apart, then slams back by the violent maw of escalating earthquakes. The brutal energy of each concussion forces the air from my lungs.

Shaken and disoriented, I slam the door shut and step across the hallway. Putting my fist on the opposite door, I lean slightly to catch my breath. But the wood beneath my hand feels hot. Really hot.

What the hell's happening here? I fling the second entryway open, and heat blasts across my body. Flames engulf the iconic English clock, Big Ben, as the hands read noon. Fire jumps to the surrounding buildings as if fueled by a powerful accelerant. Within minutes, the heart of London is a blazing inferno. On the street, men and women try to run from the escalating flames only to be engulfed.

Burnt alive.

Incinerated where they stand.

Those trapped in the buildings above must make a horrible choice—death by fire or jumping. The sickening crunch of bodies hitting the sidewalk turns my stomach, and I hurl the door shut.

I recognize a pattern of destruction here, involving two of nature's four elements. Reluctantly, I turn the third door's knob. The breathtaking lines of the Sydney Opera House in Australia have me holding my breath in fear. What ungodly action will happen next? A banshee roar precedes the fifteen-hundred-foot tsunami as it barrels inland, obliterating homes and buildings and destroying the Opera House. The sea decimates the second most populous city in Australia. The devastation shifts into high gear because a second wave, over two thousand feet tall, does what the first one didn't—submerges the continent from coast to coast.

There are no survivors.

Disheartened and sickened by grief, I close the door and tremble as I open the last one. A howling wind screams across the High Plains of Texas, pushing a mile-high wave of dust and debris. The horrific air current razes buildings like an atomic blast, sends cars end over end, and cleanses the landscape as thoroughly as a pressurized enema.

I recognize a greater force at work here as I close the fourth door and crumple to the hallway floor. I have witnessed the destruction of four alternate planet locations by the elements—earth, fire, water, and wind.

Bowing my head, I'm unable to grasp the senseless deaths of so many innocent people.

In my moment of need, a nearby door in the Hallway of Infinity opens, and a pixie-like young woman steps into the corridor. I've met Tara the Traveler before, and she had explained then that she was a spiritual overseer who monitored visitors journeying through dimensions. Her young face is wrinkled from concern, and she reaches out to touch my bare arm. "Archer, the destruction you've seen today is horrible. But the worst is yet to come. Know that there are forces in play that plan to compromise your home planet Earth and the alternate world you currently live in."

I curl my fingers into fists of rage, and my stomach churns. My psychic sense engages and affirms Tara's words. Faced with the potential destruction of everything I hold dear, what can I do? Where can I go? And who is behind all this?

Tara holds up her hand to stop my questions. "You will have answers soon. Be patient, and know God is behind you."

She turns and fades from sight, leaving me with a spinning head. I spread my hands across my rounded stomach, give my unborn child a protective embrace, and pray for his safety.

3

I FURROW MY BROW AND scrutinize the African American monolith lumbering into the Indigent City Mission soup kitchen. Led by a tiny Chihuahua with clip-on dreadlocks and a studded collar, the four-pound service dog leads its NFL linebacker lookalike around the empty tables until he stands at the serving line.

A deep premonition prickles my scalp when he looks down at me. Could this be the person Slash prophesied about over a year ago? This man is not a typical drifter who comes in for a hot meal and a place to sleep. The iris and pupil of his sightless eyes are dominated by a circular blast of blinding, Arctic white and are encircled by a thin ring of penetrating blue. He wears a tattered Army overcoat that is overkill in the West Texas summer heat and can't hide the prominent hump between his shoulder blades. Stunning mahogany hue enhances his high cheekbones, chiseled face, and shaved head, leaving me to wonder who he is and how he ended up here.

He reaches out and swallows my hand in his. "My name is Tenkiller."

I am used to paranormal manifestations, personally, as well as having been the daughter of parents involved in a government psychic espionage program. But this man in this setting with this spiritual aura whips my metaphysical radar into overdrive.

"Don't be alarmed, Archer," he rumbles in a baritone.

How the hell does he know my name?

"I have a message for you." Tenkiller reaches into his overcoat and removes a round stethoscope diaphragm, the one doctors place against a patient's chest to listen to the heart but without the rubber tubing.

Anticipating his move, I step back.

He hears my movement. "There's nothing to fear. Just let me do what I do best."

Sensing his true intention, I oblige reluctantly.

The human giant leans in, finds my left shoulder by touch, and moves the device down my chest.

The food line is empty, except for Tenkiller. A few transients sit at a corner table with cups of steaming coffee. Their conversation stops when the giant African American scowls and sweeps his sightless gaze their way. Wooden chairs scrape the floor, and the quick patter of feet mark their exit into the sunbaked street outside.

My heart thunders in my chest.

Tenkiller reaches inside his pocket, removes a thin electrical wire with small jacks on each end, and plugs one into the base of the circular device.

Then he inserts the other jack into his ear. A perfectly formed, silver-plated ear, with tiny resistors, capacitors, and a blinking red, LED light.

He takes a breath, presses the diaphragm firmly against my upper chest. "Don't be afraid."

Just as I think things can't get any more bizarre, the flashing red light turns green, and faint music drifts from his electronic connection, music that cools my senses, conveying the craggy, celestial beat of ragged, Jamaican reggae. Random words deliver a message only he can understand and ignites a smile.

A smile that quickly aborts into a frown.

He removes the diaphragm from my chest, and I stare up into his Arctic eyes.

Tenkiller clears his throat. "The delicate membrane separating good from evil has been ruptured by the devil's assault upon four planets of the multiverse. In the coming week, Satan will reign chaos upon the planet Earth and three more alternate worlds. All that stands in his way is the female triumvirate—the Sisters of Three—of which you are their chosen leader."

The Sisters of Three and chosen leader?

Under normal circumstances, I would discount his message as the raving of the mentally ill. The indigents that come to the City Mission, where I volunteer, are frequently delusional and speak of government mind control and alien abduction. Nothing about this man confirms my suspicion. My psychic appraisal reveals that there is more to him than meets the eye. For now, though, I will wait on the additional proof. After all, a lot could happen in the coming days, and the worlds will be safe until then.

I lean in and touch his arm. "Just supposing what you say is true, what evidence do you have?"

Tenkiller raises to his full height. "Yesterday, in the Hallway of Infinity, you witnessed the assault of four alternate planets. Satan's team was responsible and died with each breach.

"Tonight, at ten p.m., check your email and follow the directions." He pats my arm. "You, of all people, should know things are not always what they seem." The giant tugs the Chihuahua's leash and smiles, showing his even white teeth. "Now that we've dispensed with the unpleasantness, Rambo would prefer a bowl of sparkling water, and I'll have the soup *du jour.*"

Sparkling water?

Soup *du jour?*

At an indigent shelter?

Four worlds are targeted next, including Earth and my alternate planet, and the prophet of doom has a sense of humor. Go figure.

4

COFFIN TIME PILLOW TALK

IT WAS DARK-THIRTY, AND Tenkiller's internal clock was winding down. His vindictive service dog, Rambo, had taken the long way back to the crib, and if Tenkiller's instincts were right, it was canine intimidation, pure and simple.

He smashed the litter underfoot while counting his steps to the alley door. At eighteen paces, he mentally scanned the backstreet for human presence, found none, and then turned left. Even though he was blind, Tenkiller could sense the spiritual aura of others, both dead and alive. All too often, he spoke to the surrounding spirits, giving them encouragement and directions to find the light. A lost soul himself, he did what he could to help.

His hand brushed against the weathered doorknob, and he concentrated on the deadbolt inside. With a single thought, he snapped the interior lock open and stepped into the abandoned church that had been his home for three years.

Back when he had his sight, he scouted the location as a safe place to sleep. It wasn't much different now, just a small pulpit and seven dusty pews—a failed spiritual ministry for Amarillo, Texas's vagrants and the homeless. To those sleeping on the streets, this was a gold coin among copper pennies. So to discourage other transients from moving in, he had imprinted a negative "vibe" around the premises. A vibe that left potential intruders quaking with panic and fear. If that didn't deter them, then, the seven-foot-long coffin visible from the back door did. The casket rested in the center of the blackened pulpit and was splattered with gang graffiti and splashed with human blood.

His blood.

It was a clear message to others—stay away.

Tenkiller unleashed Rambo and raised the coffin lid.

He had stripped the original padding and satin lining until the inside was an empty shell. However, he had added a unique touch, one that screamed to the sane. He was the conductor on the crazy train. Tenkiller had glued sixty-three small radios to the inside of the casket lid and along the interior sides. If that wasn't overkill, he'd fastened a laptop and keyboard directly in front of his face to use when the coffin lid was closed.

He called it his heavenly home theatre, and when engaged, even the most snobbish audiophile would be blown away with its sound.

Rambo scratched his sleeping pad, turned around, and settled in for the night. The Chihuahua farted and then growled at Tenkiller as if challenging him to comment.

This, too, was one of his crosses to bear.

He climbed in, pulled the lid down, then closed his eyes. Cold and alone, he was ready to go home—back to his maker. But that wasn't what the higher powers had in mind. When the unplugged radios lit up, the heat from hundreds of electrical circuits raised the temperature inside his coffin.

"Ten?" Colonel Lander's voice reverberated through sixty-three shades of grey, off grey, and dark grey radios, shaking the casket, setting the stage for another dismal night.

"Son, three years ago, you were an Angel with a divine mission. A simple assignment in Amarillo. But, y'all lost yourself. Lost yourself to booze. Lost yourself to carnal desire. Pissed away whatever dignity you had left and blinded yourself from cheap liquor and sexual excess. I'm ashamed of you, Ten. You got no one to blame but yourself," his heavenly handler hammered the message home. "And make a note because I'll have more instructions for you tomorrow morning at ten, sharp."

The combined heat from sixty-three radios toasted Tenkiller like he was in Hell. And he probably would be if not for the colonel. Landers had spoken up in Ten's favor, convinced the powers that be to give him another chance.

A chance to stop the devil's machinations.

And here he was, sweating like a whore in an STD clinic, baking in his closed coffin, wishing he'd never taken that first drink three years ago.

A lot depended on Archer, and if she weren't on board the crazy train, yet, her ticket would be punched after her computer "message" tonight.

All aboard.

He turned the laptop on and twisted the top off a fifth of six-dollar Gin.

And yep, because he continued to make poor choices, Tenkiller's life was like a turd swirling down the toilet.

Totally flushed. Totally useless. Totally gone.

Until he proved differently.

5

HAVE YOU NO SHAME?

AT 9:58 THAT EVENING, I sit on my bed, in a long nightgown, laptop perched on my thighs. I turn the computer on, then watch, wait, and worry. What if Tenkiller is right? If so, am I responsible for stopping the destruction on Earth and three more alternate worlds?

A subtle sense of panic spreads like a fine mist down my chest and pools in my gut. Then it's bastard cousin, guilt, raises its hooded head and hobbles my mind. It is taunting me with what ifs? What if I choke?

What if I fail?

What if I can't save the other worlds?

A hundred thoughts hike out of a hideous hole and co-alesce into one monstrous image. Mom and Dad. Unconscious. I'm injecting the wakeup drug. Their hearts beat faster. Medical monitors scream. Vital signs flatline. Then, I learned Le Cadavre substituted a fatal dose.

Yet, I was the one who pushed the plunger. I was the one who killed them. And if I couldn't even save my parents, how can I save the four worlds?

But my parents had instilled in me a strong sense of duty—doing the right thing in spite of my doubts, in spite of my reservations, and particularly, in spite of my fear.

Getting beyond the black hole of my guilt and grief will be next to impossible.

At exactly ten p.m., an email pops up in my folder. I click twice, and an Ouija Board appears on my laptop screen. At the bottom, I read a gothic style caption.

𝕿𝖍𝖊 𝖉𝖊𝖛𝖎𝖑 𝖆𝖓𝖉 𝖍𝖎𝖘 𝖒𝖎𝖓𝖎𝖔𝖓𝖘 𝖜𝖎𝖑𝖑 𝖜𝖗𝖊𝖆𝖐 𝖍𝖆𝖛𝖔𝖈 𝖚𝖕𝖔𝖓 𝖙𝖍𝖊 𝖘𝖊𝖈𝖔𝖓𝖉 𝖘𝖊𝖙 𝖔𝖋 𝖋𝖔𝖚𝖗 𝖜𝖔𝖗𝖑𝖉𝖘.

My afternoon excursion to the first four alternate worlds barraged by the earth, fire, water, and wind comes to mind. Nine hours have elapsed since then, and the horror still echoes within my heart.

The last sentence scrolls into view, and I scan it. *What has no torso, limbs, head, or eyes, can be sent anywhere, and knows all? You have three minutes to click your answer on the Ouija Board. If you fail, the innocent's fate is in your hands.*

My eyes open wide, and I chew my bottom lip. A timer appears in the top left of the screen, and the seconds ticks by, indifferently, impersonally, and inevitably.

What the hell have I gotten into?

LYING INSIDE HIS NOW OPEN coffin, Tenkiller finished the last of his gin and let the bottle slip from his hand. It rolled off his chest, fell to the floor, and clinked against last night's empties. He had initiated the email contact with Archer, and his laptop's impersonal voice counted down, liquidating the seconds of her three-minute limit.

The heat from the sixty-three radios had dissipated, but weeks of unwashed clothes and body, bombarded by the smell of cheap gin, enhanced his sense of shame. Despite all his boozing and whoring, despite his numerous shortcomings, he still had integrity and had never lied to anyone. Not yet, but in his current situation, it wasn't a given. Tenkiller leaned over the side of his coffin and puked his guts out. He spewed the gin, all his integrity, and what little pride remained.

Unfortunately, the splatter part landed squarely on his psycho service dog, Rambo. The enraged animal jumped up from its mat, and in a fit of revenge, attacked the tip of Tenkiller's boot. Somewhere between his dry heaves and the dog's demented growling, the laptop's mechanical voice instructed, *"Press Y to continue."*

In his gin-soaked mind, Tenkiller did just that—and played into the devil's hands.

STAN WITH A POCKET PROTECTOR

STAN A WAS A DOLLAR Store man with bargain bin tastes. The fact that he was sitting on his worn couch, watching reruns of *The Golden Girls* while shoveling outdated Cheetos into his mouth, just enhanced the bland strokes of his nature. When someone asked him what the A in his name meant, he would insist it wasn't an initial. Just add it to Stan, he instructed, to reveal his true identity.

So, he'd say, engage the imagination. Mix it up.

Are you still struggling? Put the extra a after the S and get Satan. Satan with a capital S. And when thinking of the big S, an inevitable image comes to mind—seeing horns and pitchforks, now?

What isn't seen is a receding hairline. Check.

Protruding jowls. Check.

Dark rimmed bifocals that emphasized bloodshot eyes. And don't forget the packed pocket protector. Check. And double-check.

The ideal disguise when milling with mortals was to blend in. And who would suspect that an innocuous accountant was Satan?

No one, except the IRS. But, not to worry. They sold their souls a long time ago.

Stan A considered himself Chief Accountant—overseer of the ultimate ledger sheet, where lives were marked by the debits and credits earned from righteous or repugnant deeds. Being in the black bought you a berth in Heaven, where being in the red resigned your sorry ass to Hell. You break even, and maybe it's only Purgatory.

Today, mayhem and death had found their way through four worlds and would soon expand to Earth and three more planets of the multiverse.

The ultimate corporate raider had a hard-on for wholesale destruction. And nothing would stand in his way. Not God, not the Angels, and surely not Archer Wilson.

TICK-TOCK

A THOUSAND THOUGHTS PING INSIDE my mind, approaching with the speed of fright. Ninety seconds left, and the timer is rapidly funneling down to the "Oh, shit" moment. The moment when I can't answer the riddle and the "innocent's" fate slips from my hands.

Then, what happens? Will my world explode? Will the four elements wreak havoc upon all the chosen planets? Why the hell am I the selected one, the leader of the female triumvirate? Are Jacqui and Luanne the other two "sisters" as foretold by Slash over one year ago on Earth?

I try to calm my raging mind. But the riddle is inane. What doesn't have a head, torso, limbs, or eyes? And can be sent anywhere and knows everything? What kind of nonsense is that?

I take a deep breath and glance at the computer.

Forty-five seconds remain. And my heart bucks up my throat. My mouth goes dry. My mind focuses on one thing I have to protect. Something I would die to save—my unborn baby.

Thirty seconds and counting. I ignore the image of death, ignore the relentless countdown, and finally acknowledge the obvious. My child comes first, then the lives of strangers.

Twenty seconds left, and a mental edge slices the fear from my mind. An edge that delivers haunting lucidity to my thoughts.

My heart rate drops. My breath slows to an even rhythm. My mind refocuses. In a moment of brilliant clarity, the solution drops into place.

I click the Ouija Board letters with the pointer, recklessly, not bothering to think, just reacting on a primal level. Confident in my answer, three words solve the puzzle. I hit the enter button and glance at the stopped clock. One second remains. I fist punch the air and shake my head in triumph.

"What has no body, can be sent anywhere and knows everything?" The smile upon my face broadens. "My psychic ability."

LET'S HARVEST THE FRUIT

SITTING ON HIS LIVING ROOM couch, Stan had sent a request to Tenkiller's computer, and the fallen angel accepted by pressing y, granting remote access over his laptop. Moments later, Archer answered her riddle correctly and impressed Stan with her ability to think under pressure. Her last-second save impressed him but not overwhelmingly. To do that, she would have to up her game to the next level.

The accountant shoved his thick, black-rimmed glasses up with an encrusted, Cheeto-stained forefinger. He clicked a universal remote, and *The Golden Girls* flickered off the TV screen—replaced with a live feed from the farm.

The image appeared on his and Archer's laptop, originating from one of the farm's forty overhead cameras. The wide-angle view showed a stadium-sized warehouse with hundreds of nude bodies lying upon legless stainless-steel trays, suspended in place with corner connected cables that kept each human being three feet above the floor.

The "fruit," as Stan loved to call them, were all living, breathing entities. Entities without names, homeless people without someone who missed them, and in their terrorized, semi-conscious minds, they were entities without hope.

According to arrival protocol, the fresh fruit was tagged,

drugged, and laid out on a steel tray. A glucose drip was started in a vein on the left arm, while the opposing limb was tapped to capture a slow flow of lifeblood, called the harvest. Each piece of fruit had been catheterized and had a collection bag suspended beneath. A controlled climate system kept the farm at a comfortable temperature, preventing the narrowing of veins and ensuring the steady flow of blood.

Stan was CEO of the farm, a Limited Liability Company that bombarded the airwaves with a revolutionary weight loss powder, twenty-four hours a day.

Stan initiated Skype contact with Archer and said, "Congratulations. You solved the riddle!"

Archer shot back, *"Who are you? And what are these people on my screen?"*

"My name is Stan A, and you're looking at the 'farm.'"

"Is this some sick joke?"

"No. My team is milking a freakin' cash cow to the tune of a million dollars a month."

"WTF. This is crazy!"

"Not to the couch potatoes who watch my Counting Calories infomercial. They buy my product—a powdered concoction refined from harvested blood that supplies all the vital nutrients for a human body, keeps you pepped up and energized, and guarantees rapid weight loss as long as you drink three shakes a day."

Archer looked visually shaken, *"Do the words, illegal, immoral and insane register on your radar? Because, as soon as I leave, I'm going to the police, the FBI, and every other alphabet agency that'll get in line for a piece of your ass!"*

"Already. Anticipated. That. So, on to plan B."

Archer was silent.

"The farm is somewhere in the multiverse. It could be Earth or any one of an infinite number of worlds. The possibility of you stumbling across it is less than possible. Closer to improbable. No, make that fucking *impossible!"*

"You can't stop me now."

"Give me a minute, and I'll change your mind." Stan punched in the camera coordinates on his remote and brought up two young women laid out on adjacent trays. "Look close, Archer, and tell me if you recognize your two friends, Jacqui Chen and Luanne Martinez. They're your classmates from Costas's student training program, and I opened a portal between Earth and this alternate planet to bring them to my farm. But more importantly, they are the two members of the female triumvirate. The same coalition prophesied by recently discovered scrolls in the Middle East—the Three Sisters who will meddle in my affairs."

Archer fisted her hand. *"You will not see me coming. Because I will hunt you, I will find you, and I will squeeze the life from your worthless body unless you free Jacqui and Luanne, unharmed, in twenty-four hours."*

"Do you have any idea who you're threatening?" Spittle flew from Stan's mouth.

"I smelled the stink of sulfur when you told me your name. Stan A. Any fool could figure that out—anyone with half a brain and a third-grade education. So, listen close, Satan, you're going to have to put on your big boy underwear because you're dealing with the leader of the Triumvirate, and when you play with the big dogs, someone always gets hurt!"

MY HANDS SHAKE AS I power the laptop down and watch the screen go blank. A painful thud in my chest hammers out my fear, and sweat creeps up my back. I take a shaky breath and tremble with anxiety. My two friends are captive, and I will do anything to free them.

Yet, in an insane act of one-upmanship, I just threatened the supreme source of all evil and gave him the ultimatum to release

Jacqui and Luanne. I have no way in hell to find them, follow through with my threat, or finish what I started.

That is, until, a devilishly simple solution comes to mind.

9

A SLOW SEXUAL SIZZLE

WHEN TENKILLER CLIMBED OUT OF his coffin that morning, the first thing he noticed was the penetrating smell of dog poop. The next thing that registered in his gin-infused hung-over mind was the soft, slimy squish between his toes. Cold and gritty and entirely disgusting, Rambo had retaliated for last night's puke-a-thon, taking canine retribution to another level.

The fallen angel grabbed his sock and scraped the mess from between his toes. Reaching for his boot, he pulled it on, but, cool air unexpectedly flowed across the top of his foot. He leaned forward. Touched it. Realized the damn dog chewed the tip off last night.

"Son of a bitch," he muttered, careful not to add another transgression by using God's name in vain. The four-pound Rambo snarled in response as if begging him to cross the line.

But, Tenkiller wasn't in the mood for a confrontation and finished dressing. He jerked the dog's leash and drug the yapping Chihuahua across the floor, out into the alley. Then he put his shoulder behind the door and slammed it shut. The sound echoed in the air as he used his mind to close the inside lock.

Blessed with a canny, internal clock, he knew he had thirty

minutes to get something to eat and return to the crib for Colonel Landers's new instructions. But that changed when he hit the street across from the Indigent City Mission.

"Hey, Ten?"

Her sultry voice stopped him cold and stimulated his senses into a slow, sexual sizzle.

He knew the approaching click of her six-inch stilettos, the silken swish of inner thigh against thigh, the floral scent of her perfume.

Charity stopped in front of him, took his hand, and guided it over her body, in deference to his blindness. Tenkiller felt her leather miniskirt, with matching police hat, along with a sturdy riding crop and silver skull earrings.

He had met her on the streets one night, years ago, after being kicked out of Snake's Sixth Street Bar. And, yeah, once a week, for the last three years, he knew Charity in every sense of the word.

Physically.

Mentally.

And Biblically.

After her calculated tease, the sexual sizzle of moments ago escalated into a full-fledged, figure-feeling, tactile seduction, which left him lightheaded and weak-kneed. Rambo gave a high-pitched yip and spoiled the moment when Tenkiller felt something running over his exposed toes.

Something warm.

Something wet.

Charity released his hand and gave a throaty laugh. "I knew you were kinky, Ten, but a toe fetish, a golden shower, *and* a Chihuahua? I don't see that combination until the bars let out on Saturday night. It's refreshing that you're exploring your sexuality."

She gave him a solid swat on the butt with her riding crop, leaned close, and pressed her moistened lips against his ear.

"Traffic on the street won't pick up for a few more hours. Why don't we go to my house and have a drink?"

Even though the morning was still cool, Tenkiller began to sweat as he imagined the morning's first alcohol. "I don't have the money. For the gin."

She grabbed his crotch—gave it an appreciative squeeze. "With a package like that, I should treat you."

He licked his lips, oblivious to his urine-soaked toes, unaware of the staring commuters, heedless of his meeting in thirty minutes.

"Well," Charity whispered, "if you're worried about the money, it's on me."

The hooker took his hand.

The devil took another slice of Ten's soul.

The fallen angel took a turn toward the toll road of intoxication. And, if he could see, he knew it would be the scenic route.

10

TEN YEARS MINIMUM, TWENTY MAX

LEE KALE JERKED THE IGNITION hot wires apart on his piece of shit '78, Gremlin, and the engine shuddered to a halt. He parked on the outer edge of the Clements Unit's parking lot, the TDCJ maximum-security prison where the worst of the worst in the Lone Star State were housed.

He shoved the horror of what he was about to do back into its dark hole because, within the next hour, he would use his position as a unit mailman to help free Jason Blaine—the vicious, prison overlord of three hundred serial murderers, rabid Neo-Nazis, and other extremist criminals.

And, after that, Lee would forget this ever happened.

But if he backed out, his infant son would die.

He checked his watch. 7:45 a.m. Fueled by fear, his heartbeat drummed from desperation as he opened the Gremlin's door to what might be the last free day of his life. At twenty-four, he should be enjoying himself, not facing the extermination of his young son.

A week ago, late Sunday night, an anonymous caller told him to step onto his back porch. Lee put the phone down, opened the door, then puked when he saw a deer blatantly slaughtered on his deck. A bloody message, smeared on the wall above, warned. Cooperate. Or else. From inside the home, he heard his one-year-old son crying, and Lee forced himself to walk past the deer and back into the kitchen. His hand shook as he picked up the receiver. The caller brutally made his point and told Lee exactly what he needed to do.

He should have gone to the police then. But there was one detail he didn't want the authorities to know. Lee was heavily in debt to an organized crime loan shark. His mother had stage four pancreatic cancer and needed chemo. Lee was in over his head and had no way to pay the $30,000 back. Until he got the call—an offer to forgive his debt. All he had to do was help Jason Blaine escape. Before he hung up, the voice on the phone added a terrifying incentive to ensure Lee's participation. "Imagine your son in place of the deer."

He clenched his fists and trudged across the pavement. After this fiasco was over, he would get a job somewhere else. Anything would beat working amid the most violent criminals in the state. Anything.

He entered the security checkpoint and queued up behind ten employees waiting to be screened. Lee adopted a passive demeanor and prayed for luck. As he had anticipated, the guards were doing quick pat downs to speed up the line. When he got to the x-ray machine, Lee removed his shoes, emptied his pockets, and took off his belt. Placing the items in a plastic tray, he set it on the conveyor belt and got in line for the metal detector. The small pill he was carrying for offender Blaine would bring on severe convulsions, with enough severity for an ambulance ride to the local hospital. The introduction of illicit drugs into a maximum security facility was a felony offense with harsh sentencing guidelines. So Lee had tucked it securely in his underwear between his *dos amigos.*

He stepped through the opening of the screening device, and the damned detector dinged, halting the line behind him. When the officer motioned him forward, his heart did a triple tap tango across his chest.

"Over here." The guard grinned. "And spread 'em."

Sweat beaded on his forehead, and his stomach cramped. He submitted to the pat-down on legs, arms, chest, and back before the officer dug into Lee's pocket.

The guard swung a set of keys from his fingertips. "You forgot something. Back up and go through again," he pointed toward the metal detector.

Lee cleared the machine this time and quickly gathered his shoes and belongings.

A few minutes later, he handed his prison ID through a slot to another officer behind bulletproof glass and passed through two massive steel doors. Once outside, the guard returned the ID, and Lee hurried through a chain-link gate. Rows of razor wire layered across the top of the fence glinted in the morning sun.

By now, his armpits had created a small sweat stain, and perspiration dotted his forehead. He prayed no one would notice because he wasn't a good enough liar to deflect their questions. When he glanced at the perimeter guard towers, his heart thundered into a guilty rhythm. These positions were staffed by emotionless men who would shoot to kill anyone trying to escape.

Technically he wasn't trying to escape, but that did little to still his anxiety. He was here to make sure someone got out. Lee imagined his head in the crosshairs of a high-powered rifle and could almost hear the shooter exhale as his finger tightened against the trigger.

Guilt was an emotional carnivore, but survival was the apex predator. When Lee reached the admin entrance, survival had muted his misgivings. But, it did nothing for the hollow, empty hole in his soul.

His legs barely moved, like slogging through deep water. In a mental fog, he plodded down a sterile, gray hallway until he turned in to the mail room. A few coworkers looked up, said,

"Hello," as he passed by. His stomach knotted tighter, and his heart did cardiac kicks inside his chest. It took all his will power to act normal as he mumbled, "Back at ya." Lee grabbed his rolling buggy loaded with unopened legal correspondence and packages bound for the High-Security offenders.

He pushed the cart into the hallway, looked around, and took a tentative breath of relief. Lee leaned into the buggy, willing himself to move faster. But when he turned the corner, his supervisor unexpectedly stopped him with a firm hand on his arm. "Lee, the warden and the High-Security major want to see you."

Panic sunk its fangs deep in his chest, and he fought to keep from screaming, "What's going on?" To his ears, the three words sounded drawn out, elongated, incomprehensible. His heart spiked up his throat with unforgiving, steel hooks. Guilt shredded his mind. How could they know about Jason Blaine? Had he been set up?

The supervisor appeared indifferent. "Don't know, but they've been here for half an hour."

Lee wiped his forehead.

When the warden of the maximum security unit wanted to see you, that was bad news. But add the High-Security major, and that was a double-damned dilemma.

The supervisor grabbed the buggy and turned it around. "I'll park it until you finish." He nodded toward the conference room.

"Until you finish" could mean just that, a simple conversation and nothing else. Or, it could mean he'd be finished in the next five minutes. Like, welcome to the rapist romper room, a euphemism for the prison showers—the same place where sadistic felons played hide-the-sausage.

Lee shuddered. He knew where the sausage would go.

For the next ten to twenty years.

He took a deep breath and entered the room, forcing himself to look them in the eye. A clock on the wall ticked loudly, the air conditioner kicked in, and two hardened prison officials calmly stared him down.

"You wanted to see me?"

"Have a seat." The warden patted the chair placed between him and the Major. "We have something to discuss."

FROM DEEP WITHIN
COMES STRENGTH

WHEN LEE KALE SAW THE warden of the most notorious maximum security unit in Texas sitting with his High-Security major, he nearly pissed himself. But, he sucked it up, squeezed his legs together, and slid onto the metal folding chair. The overhead fluorescent light hummed, and his heart pounded like a jackrabbit caught between two vicious wolves. He forced himself to glance at the stone-faced men.

They grimaced.

He imagined two predator's jaws opening wide and exposing wet, deadly canines, seconds from ripping through his neck.

His left eye twitched. The wall clock sliced the seconds away. Brutally. Impersonally. It seemed the obliteration of time mocked his last moments as a free man.

Lee glanced down at his crotch where he had hidden offender Blaine's pill and caught the warden observing him.

In the silence of the room, he heard the steady rhythm of their breathing, punctuated by the clock liquidating his remaining life.

Both men moved closer, and for the first time, Lee summoned the courage to look up, reading the message on their faces.

Expressions without compassion. Without forgiveness. Without mercy.

The ferocious clarity of his position slammed home. He was so screwed. His heart power humped the inside of his chest. The pain of discovery accelerated his breath. Did they know? What other reason could they call him in for? He racked his brain, looking for a glimmer of hope, and sat on his hands to stop their trembling. Lee was a heartbeat away from spilling his guts. But, spilling his guts wouldn't keep his baby boy alive. He alone would see that this nightmare ended with what the anonymous caller wanted—offender Blaine's freedom. Lee would lie and cheat and steal. He would do whatever it took to save his child. Emerging from deep in his gut, calmness appeared, flushing the burn of fear from his face and straightening his spine.

He looked the warden in the eye. "What did you want to talk about, sir?"

DON THE ARMOR

THE WARDEN STROKED HIS MUSTACHE and turned his chair toward Lee. "We came across some information concerning you in High Security. Two days ago, Officer Colby intercepted a note from an unknown offender who was passing it to another cell. As soon as Colby read it, he relayed it to Major Gordon."

Lee wasn't going to let them see him sweat. But pissing his pants wasn't out of the question. "What does this have to do with me?" The warden moved closer, and Lee smelled onions on his breath. Saw a shred of meat in the gap between his teeth.

For the first time since he entered the room, both men smiled. The change in emotion confused Lee. But, his gut whispered that maybe this wasn't about offender Blaine.

"I'll let Major Gordon explain the note." The warden patted Lee's leg. "And for the record, you're not in any trouble."

The sudden release of anxiety halted his trembling, and Lee exhaled. The High-Security major shifted in his chair. "We suspect the threat came from Jason Blaine, who is trying to enlist the Aryan Brotherhood to take you out."

Thoughts bombarded Lee's mind, but the overriding feeling was relief. They didn't know about the pill. In a microsecond, he saw the work of the anonymous caller and thought what better way to deflect his involvement in Blaine's escape. In the warden and major's eyes, why would Blaine try to kill Lee if he was helping the offender escape? The knot in the mailman's stomach unclenched—this was a turn in his favor. He moved his hands onto his lap and decided to play along with their theory. "Staff death threats are a common occurrence in prison. Being killed by a convict isn't guaranteed. So, I intend to use my wits and be careful."

Lee's lies were coming easier. "Why would Blaine want to kill me?"

The warden furrowed his brow. "I've done my homework on you. The word among the officers and our offender 'insiders,' is that you're incorruptible. You have a good reputation. You're by the book."

The mailman took a deep breath, managing to look grateful.

Major Gordon lifted a black body armor vest off the floor. "I expect you to wear this every time you deliver in High Security."

The warden nodded in agreement. "It's possible that Blaine wants someone else delivering the mail. Someone he can corrupt."

Both men stood, and the tension broke—their meeting was over.

The "incorruptible" Lee shook their hands and left the room. On the way to his mail buggy, he knew that if he'd told the truth, the wolves would have ripped his throat out.

He touched his neck and smiled.

Team Lee: 6. Team Carnivore: 0.

DON'T FLUSH TWICE

IN THE PRIVACY OF THE High-Security men's room, Lee removed Blaine's knock-out pill and put it in his right pocket next to the paperclip. The anonymous caller had said the drug would induce unconsciousness and severe convulsions, requiring an ambulance ride to the hospital. In three to four hours, the effect would dissipate, and Blaine would awaken while handcuffed to his hospital bed. Prison procedure required a guard to be stationed outside the room, which would allow Blaine the privacy to retrieve the paperclip from his rectum, bend it, and pick the lock on his cuffs.

Lee left the men's room and pushed his buggy down a narrow walkway, past a window that revealed the electronic control center for High Security. Three guards watched a bank of closed-circuit television monitors for six pods, home to over three-hundred seasoned criminals. The metal door at the end of the walkway clanked open by a hidden chain drive and then closed behind him as he passed into the holding area. This thirty by thirty-foot enclosure held eight small, one-man cells, with seven offenders who were in the process of relocation within High Security.

The guard behind the glass nodded. Another metal door opened. Lee entered a straight arterial walkway that extended for twenty yards. The six pods were evenly spaced on both sides of the passage. Alpha pod, which housed offender Blaine, was Lee's first stop. His heart rate accelerated as he pressed the call button and glanced up at the CCTV camera. The intercom crackled, and a guard acknowledged his presence. "All hell broke loose in Alpha pod fifteen minutes ago. The tear gas ain't fully dispersed, so be prepared."

When the access door opened, Lee's eyes immediately teared up, his throat tightened as he breathed in, and his nose gushed a thick mucus. Instinctively coughing, then gasping for air, he sounded like an asthmatic in desperate need of his inhaler. Lee leaned into his buggy, violently purging his lungs to the point of almost vomiting. He shuffled toward the floor fan, where the fresh air allowed him to breathe again.

The pod had a narrow, open walkway that ran for thirty yards and divided fifteen cells on the left from fifteen cells on the right. In the center of the concrete aisle was a small metal table for the guards. Four stationary seats allowed the officers a place to sit during their twelve-hour shifts.

Each cell was eight by twelve feet and housed two offenders. On most days, the warm body count totaled sixty per pod and presented an institutional nightmare when they misbehaved.

In the year he had worked there, Lee quickly learned not to look into the offender's cells, unless they called him with a question. Prison etiquette, even among murderers and serial criminals, was expected. Noncompliance brought severe consequences. The message was clear. If you didn't want feces or urine thrown on you, respect their privacy.

Another dark perspective of prison life presented itself when Lee passed an open cell. A white-garbed trustee sloshed his mop across the floor, using a harsh disinfectant and cleaner to dilute a massive pool of blood on the concrete pad. The inhumanity of living in a maximum security prison often led to insanity, other times, suicide. By the large amount of blood, an offender had traded his misery here for a permanent place in Hell.

Lee was about fifteen feet from the guard's table when a steady flow of water gushed along the left walkway. He stayed to the right and recognized another type of rebellion by the bored offenders. Offenders who plugged their toilets, defecated and urinated in them, then continually flushed until the pungent eliminations found their way onto the walkway. It was an irritant to the guards, but Lee thought about the cell where it started. Two stupid bastards had to walk in it, smell it. If they kept their mouths open long enough talking about it, they would taste the fruit of their efforts.

"Hey, Mailman," shouted an offender down the row. "How'd you like some of this?"

Lee looked and quickly turned away. An obese convict masturbated in front of his cell's small vertical window.

The felon laughed insanely. "See anything you like?"

Officer Dillon met Lee on the dry part of the walkway. "You wanna write him a case, Lee? Put that asshole on commissary restriction." Dillon gripped his baton. "Been waiting to bust his chops. Buncha crazy animals in here today."

Lee shook his head no. "Probably sold his psych meds for a pack of Ramen noodles. He goes nuts without them."

He stopped at the guard table, signed the log, and glanced down the row toward Blaine's cell. "Got books and legal for the bad boy in one twelve."

"Blaine, huh? For some reason, he's actually behaving today. Not like him. When things get quiet, it's like Friday the thirteenth. Pretty soon something bad's gonna happen."

The guard followed Lee to the cell and stopped. Both men waited for the offender to come to the door. Lee reached over and got the legal letter from the buggy. "ID, name, and number."

Blaine answered, and Lee verified his identity from the information on the envelope. After a quick look at the convict's ID, the mailman took his Bic pen, slid it inside the flap, and ripped the letter open.

"Almost forgot the books," Lee stepped back, giving the officer room to open the food slot in the middle of the cell door.

"Blaine, I want your ass five feet from the door." The guard motioned with his hand.

"Whatever you say, Boss." The offender shuffled backward.

Lee was at a moral crossroad now. Two lives hang in the balance. Without hesitation, he chose the path that allowed him and his son to live.

The mailman handed Dillon four books for inspection. While the guard thumbed through them for hidden contraband, Lee palmed the pill and paperclip from his pocket and removed the three-page legal document from Blaine's attorney.

Dillon opened the next book and whistled. *"Penthouse Letters.* Whew, wee. It seems we got *Volume II, Prison Pen Pal Lovers.* I tell ya, Blaine, the only love you'll get in here is from Rosy. Rosy palm."

While the officer stared at the text, Lee made his move. He held the legal letter in his left hand, hid the pill and paperclip in his right. A glance at the guard and Lee dropped the contraband inside the cell door, out of Dillon's sight.

Or so he thought.

The pill landed inside, but the damned paperclip caught on the edge of the food slot opening.

Lee looked up at the officer.

Dillon's eyes darkened, and he jerked Lee's left hand. "Mailman, you're about to fuck up, big time."

Caught in the headlights, Lee was not ready to be tied, tried, and fried by the criminal justice system. Yet, his life was over now, his son's death guaranteed. And he was almost there, nearly finished with this mission from Hell. Lee had failed. Miserably.

Officer Dillon pointed to the top of Blaine's legal correspondence. There in plain sight was a paperclip holding the pages together. "Can't have shit like that in Blaine's hands, can we? No telling what he could do with that."

The mailman removed the metal clip and pushed the letter through the food slot while brushing the first paperclip onto the cell floor. He dropped the correspondence inside the door and followed it with the four books.

The guard closed the slot and patted Lee's shoulder. "If that's the worst thing you do all day, then everything else will be downhill."

Offender Blaine moved up to the cell window and smiled—a sick, twisted grin, punctuated by empty, haunted eyes. Eyes that promised extreme violence. He was in his late thirties, stood erect, and was stripped to the waist, proudly displaying offensive tattoos of Nazi SS insignia, a portrait of Adolph Hitler, and an Iron Cross. On either side of his shaved head were matching swastikas.

Lee backed up—the raw presence of pure evil reached through the prison door, violating his sense of safety.

Blaine's eyes took on a malicious glow. "I'll see you and your son later, Mailman. And when I do, it'll go downhill from there."

A ball of fear squirmed in the mailman's stomach, gutting the hope that he had fulfilled his obligation. He thought about his mother and her fight against cancer. His life was like a game with five seconds left in the fourth quarter. The center snapped the ball. The quarterback's pass was in the air, gliding over the opponent's heads, spot on to the running back in the end zone. The clock had one second left as the receiver reached out to catch it. A buzzer sounded just as an opposing player deflected the ball, ending the game with a cruel defeat. The final score? *Team Lee: 0. Team Nazi: 6.*

He had bet his and his son's lives on a dangerous gambit. He had delivered on his debt, and the psychopathic felon threatened his life. But, above all, he had to make damned sure Jason Blaine was either back in prison or dead before he harmed anyone else.

14

ALRIGHT, ALRIGHT, ALRIGHT

I SETTLE INTO MY ALTERNATE parents' recliner with both feet up and a stuffed backpack at my side. After a glance at the living room clock, I determine half of my twenty-four-hour ultimatum to Stan A is gone. Intuitively, I knew he wasn't going to release my two friends. Because the devil had taunted me with the impossibility of finding the "farm," it is time to turn up the gas, toss his freakin' ass in the fire, and wait for the snap, crackle, and sizzle of frying flesh.

To do that, I rely upon a deduction I cultivated to fruition. The key to the mystery is our internet communication last night. If Stan was in a different world than mine, we couldn't have connected on the web. As a result, the "farm" is not at some remote point in the multiverse.

My two captive friends are here in this alternate earth—the same one where I live with my new parents and fiancé, Slash.

Months ago, when I first projected my consciousness to another world, I encountered Tara the Traveler, a spiritual monitor, who oversees visitors journeying through the dimensions. Tara had explained the planets of the multiverse were like an infinite number of tiny bubbles. Bubbles that were but a heartbeat apart, with each one separate and autonomous of the others. But, Tara warned, if a portal, or rift, occurred between two worlds, devastating changes would destroy the breached planets.

I shudder, remembering the destruction visited upon four worlds yesterday and suspect Stan might have opened a passage between them or introduced a high-tech weapon.

When Allen Costas, my dead parents' boss and director of psychic espionage, was still alive, he had established links with three different planets in order to loot their treasures. But I was on his trail and narrowly closed the portals in time, averting destruction.

The reason behind the violent planetary repulsion is that each world in the multiverse has a different gravitational signature. Instead of the alternate planets attracting each other as the earth and moon do, they would drive each other apart. It is imperative to sever the link within twenty-four hours because the proximity and discordant energy between the opposing worlds would result in devastation.

I push the theory from my mind and think of my physical body back on Earth. My astral spirit resides in my doppelganger in this alternate world, so if Satan destroys Earth and my adopted planet, I would have to look for another home. The thought of being alone is frightening and really depresses me, so I concentrate on my secret weapon. Using my ultimate psychic power, I will stop time at the farm and rescue my friends. After the two girls are safe, I will shove a bucket of whoop-ass down Stan's throat and deliver a personal message to the devil—whenever you step off the porch, you don't fuck with the big dogs because someone always gets hurt.

15

PLAN B

I GRAB MY BACKPACK, GRIT my teeth, and get ready to go. Standing in my parents' living room, I visualize the doorway at the heart of time and think the three words that will start my journey.

Time, time, time.

I transport immediately into the Time Guardian's living room and race across the floor. Flinging the door open, I sprint down the Hallway of Infinity—led by my intuition to the third beige entryway on my right. I grip the doorknob, take a deep breath, and step inside of Stan A's farm.

The door clicks shut behind me, and I wipe the sweat from my brow before uttering, *"Prohibere tempus."* These two words effectively stop time within the facility. The vast amphitheater called the farm is a visual obscenity, lined with stainless steel tables of the living dead. My stomach squirms, my pulse pounds, and my rage rocks off the scale. Hundreds of innocent men and women are bleeding to death for Stan A's financial gain.

Knowing the devil enjoys the traumatized state of his fruit, it is possible that his victims are on the border of sedation and consciousness so that he can feed off their terror and horror.

I open myself psychically, tune in to the victim's collective consciousness, and sense overpowering fear. A mental knife honed upon their suffering lances my heart.

Wrath rises in a hot, violent flush, spread up my neck and face. I clench my fists, take a faltering breath, and desperately scan the facility for my two friends.

The amphitheater is laid out like a large city block and divided into four squares, where each one holds approximately seventy-five bodies. Since my friends are unconscious, it will be difficult to locate them with my intuition. If I were to walk each section, it would take hours to find Jacqui and Luanne. Yet, I am prepared and dig a pair of binoculars out of my knapsack. Climbing on top of a nearby desk, I raise the field glasses to my eyes and focus on each quadrant, efficiently and effectively—and sigh with relief when I ID the two women in the furthest section.

I take off at a trot and remember the three instances when I stopped time, which lasted between twelve to fifteen minutes. Since my psychic gift didn't come with a manual, I am uncertain of how long I have before time lurches back into motion and exposes me.

Operating on the assumption that less is best, I'm going to try and hold my clock freezing exposure to ten minutes. It is imperative to get my two friends out now because they could be bled to death before I return.

During Stan A's live feed from the farm last night, I had noticed large rolling gurneys along the outer wall surrounding the four sections. I surmise they were used to transport new victims to the steel tables as well as remove the dead.

I run to the fourth square's outer wall, grab a cart, and weave my way around the frozen attendants. As I race down the concrete pathway leading to my two friends, the immobile workers appear to have been making adjustments to the drugs feeding into their captive's IVs.

The twisted perversion of the farm compounded by the

innocent victim's suffering is cruelty incarnate. I swear to take Stan's sorry ass down and grind his face in broken glass for the next eternity. But, that will wait for another place, another time. For now, I position the cart parallel to the metal table, holding Jacqui Chen's body, then, remove her sedation IV, the blood collection apparatus, as well as the catheterization tube. I use an overhead hydraulic lift to move the unconscious woman onto the cart before moving to Luanne. Finally, I disconnect my second friend and transfer her beside Jacqui.

I breathe heavily and wipe the sweat on my brow. Both women are completely nude and remain motionless while I tighten their webbed body straps, securing them to the cart. Starting the task of rolling two-hundred-fifty pounds of dead weight across the concrete amphitheater, I scan the farm for an exit.

That is plan A.

Plan B, getting them to safety, is still a bit murky.

I glance at my watch and realize it stopped when I entered the facility. A quick estimate puts me inside for twenty minutes—ten minutes past my limit Yet, all the farm's workers and hundreds of harvested victims are still eerily quiet, frozen in place by my strange gift.

Tara the Traveler had explained how my ability to stop time was a latent talent, which had awakened when Allen Costas put me in a hypnotic trance months ago on Earth.

If I had known Costas and Le Cadavre would be behind my parents' and fiancé's deaths, I would have wasted their sorry asses when I stopped time in their office.

For a moment, I relive the illusion of "what if." What if I hadn't injected my parents with a death-inducing drug? What if I had been able to save Slash? But, the delusion of "what if" can't change the reality of my life. I killed my mother and father. Slash, indirectly murdered by Costas, died in my arms. Even though I had reconnected with my alternate loved ones in a parallel world, it isn't the same. It just doesn't feel right and never relieved my guilt over their deaths at Costas's facility.

I guide the rolling cart down an arterial path dividing the four quadrants in half. For the next few minutes, I put one foot ahead of the other until I look up and see an exit sign above a doorway.

My lips lift into a grin. My spirits raise, but then, the unthinkable happens. The farm's workers begin to move as if awakened from a deep sleep. Time reasserts itself.

It's time to haul ass and get my friends out of this house of horror, now.

I swing the cart around a stirring technician and approach the exit behind him. Pushing the trolley up to the door, I ram it open. Outside, the afternoon sun illuminates a small whirlwind that swirls dust across the walkway leading to the employee parking lot.

I step quickly, wheel the two women outside, and slam the door shut. Then silently pray for their safety.

Planning has always been my forte, and I anticipate problems. In preparation for today, I brought six wooden wedges and a hammer tucked in my backpack. My pulse thunders in my ears as I pound the wood in the crack between the door frame and the door, wedging the exit shut.

Grabbing the gurney, I roll Jacqui and Luanne down the sidewalk and onto the asphalt parking lot. The next part of Plan B is to get a ride out of here.

Quickly.

I avoid the newer vehicles with their advanced security features until I see an older pickup parked on the edge of the lot. I wheel the women behind it, open the tail end of the truck, and push the top part of the hydraulic gurney over the suspended tailgate until its wheels fold underneath. Then, I shove the cart down the truck bed until it hits the end of the cab and place a tarp lying in the back over my nude friends.

Finally, I hook three bungee cords in eyelets along both sides of the bed floor, crossing over the girl's bodies, to keep the gurney from moving.

I slam the tailgate shut, rush to the driver's door, and pull the handle. When it fails to open, I backhand the glass with the hammer, shattering the window into tiny pebbles. Clearing the frame of loose fragments, I reach inside, unlock the vehicle, and jump into the cab. The ignition switch is on the right side of the steering column, and I smash the metal encasement until it breaks off. Using a small pair of metal cutters, I sever the exposed wiring.

Sweat rolls down my face, and I concentrate on stripping the hot wires. Just as I finish the first one, a siren shrieks inside the farm. Angry voices carry from behind the blocked exit, across the parking lot, and through the truck's broken window. The yelling stops, and the frantic thump of bodies against the wedged door screams my time is running out.

I look up just as the door bursts open, and an angry mob of technicians rushes out. The impossible thought spurs me to say, *"Prohibere tempus."* For whatever reason, the men keep running toward me, and I can't stop time again so soon.

They are forty feet away, and I focus on the one uniformed guard carrying a handgun. He barks orders and directs the technicians to search the lot.

My fingers tremble. They haven't seen me yet. I peel the last bit of insulation away, take a deep breath, and touch the wires together.

The starter doesn't engage.

I spark the wires again. Nothing but a *click.*

On the third try, the engine turns over.

And over.

And over.

The guard is five cars away, head turning until he reacts to the sound.

He begins running.

Two cars away, we lock eyes.

I pump the gas pedal like crazy.

He raises his handgun.

Aims at my head.

A bullet shatters the passenger's window, and Plan B hemorrhages into pure chaos.

16

X-RATED ANGEL

TENKILLER FELT HIS WAY OUT of the hooker's kitchen and stumbled across the cracked linoleum into her living room. Her low rent, ranch house rambler allowed the noontime sunlight in through the open window and began to warm his chilled body. When the cumulative effect of too many cigarettes and too much reefer caused him to cough, he nearly hacked up a lung. A pint of gin was gone, too, guzzled down by Tenkiller.

The angel swayed from side to side and knew the ride inside Charity's Carnal Cavern was over. His body ached, so he stretched upward, nearly touched the ceiling, and fell on his butt with a loud *whump.*

His sexual encounter had started one hour ago with a spine-tingling kiss, led to erotic grinding, and gave rise to a raging erection. In the heat of passion, he ripped his clothes off, shredded his self-respect, and pissed away a ten a.m. commitment with Colonel Landers.

The beads hanging over the dungeon's exit rustled as Charity entered the living room. He felt her body heat and heard her scoot his torn shirt and pants into a pile with her foot.

"If you hadn't been in such a hurry to get 'em off, you'd have something to wear." She swatted him on the thigh with her riding crop as he got up, then pushed his Army surplus coat into his hands. "This'll get you back to your crib until you get some new clothes."

Tenkiller sensed her sated, languid energy—took pride that she was satisfied with their "session." Charity traced her fingertip across his stomach. "I assume you have something else to wear?"

"Not exshactly." Tenkiller weaved as he tugged the knee length coat on and adjusted the collar to hide the hump at the base of his neck. "Thish is all I've got."

Voices from a neighbor's yard filtered through the walls, and she moved closer, rubbed her body against his, and whispered, "Ten, I've never seen anyone with a sex drive like yours. You're one horny little devil."

Tenkiller cringed.

Guilt escalated within his gin-infused mind.

In a moment of self-awareness, he knew his breath smelled like a pile of sunbaked baby shit. His body smelled like sex and stale sweat. And if he could have smelled his pickled brain, it would reek of cheap gin.

When Charity told him he was "one horny little devil," it sparked a feeling he had tried his best to avoid.

Shame.

Over three years ago, he had an angelic mission.

Tears welled up in his eyes. Condemnation spread like cancer in his gut. He swayed, on the verge of passing out.

The horrific memory of his failure breached his mental defenses. He pictured the innocent people that died.

Despair from his negligence had led to his decadent decline, and now the sexual reference to the horny devil inside him twisted the blade on too many levels.

It was harsh.

It was cruel.

But it was so true.

Tenkiller hung his head, put on his boots, and grabbed his shredded clothes from the floor. When he called Rambo, the neurotic refugee from the dog pound didn't growl at him, didn't piss on him, and didn't try to intimidate him for his weakness.

If the service chihuahua could have talked, it might have put things differently. But, for now, Tenkiller needed the illusion of compassion.

However far he'd fallen in the eyes of God, he felt an ember of goodness. Goodness that still glowed within. And he prayed that spark would take hold and consume him before the alcohol, drugs, and sex did.

Tenkiller wiped his face and meekly followed Rambo out the door. Back into the cesspool of a life he'd created. The noontime traffic buzzed past him. The exhaust fumes burned his lungs, and the hot sidewalk baked his booted feet.

A dangerous tingle started at the base of his spine, moving up his back and across his shoulders. An unconscious impulse guided his right hand into the Army coat's pocket, and a prickle of excitement aborted his better judgment. He touched a pint of gin he had purchased last night.

One twist and the cap came off.

The blood raced in his veins.

He brought it to his lips.

The first pull was pure joy.

And the keen edge of shame began to fade.

He took another swig.

And then one more.

In a moment of profound loss, the hunger to do the right thing subsided. The noise of the city muted. His world became the gin.

And when that was gone, so was he.

As he shuffled behind a tiny oxymoron named Rambo, warm tears rolled down his cheeks, and he cried for the angel he should have been.

17

DON'T TURN LEFT, TURN TO WHAT'S LEFT

TENKILLER PAUSED IN FRONT OF his alleyway door and mentally snapped the inside lock open. When he stepped over the threshold onto the pulpit, he sensed another presence.

Rambo growled once, deep and guttural.

The fallen angel had a visitor. A visitor who could enter his locked crib and not be deterred by the negative vibe Tenkiller had imprinted around the premises. A visitor who had taken the time to manifest in a human form.

That person was Colonel Landers, and when he cleared his throat, Tenkiller's last visual memory of his angelic handler manifested within.

Even though he had been blind for three years, the details were as fresh as yesterday's recollection. White linen suit and shirt. Shoulder length silver hair swept back from a prominent forehead. Penetrating eyes that absorbed more than the physical. Eyes that weighed the very essence of your soul.

If the colonel were a simple man, he might have lacked depth. But Landers was like a Russian nesting doll. Lift the first lid, and you find another doll inside. Open that one—another version. His outer layer represented a unique personality that was hard and gruff, but deep within, it was a personal warmth and caring attitude.

Everything the colonel had done for him over the years heralded a solid center of unconditional love and honor. Tenkiller was aware of the respect and unshakeable belief Landers had for him, even though he had yet to turn his life around.

All that made this meeting quite uncomfortable.

"Son, you gotta get off the booze," Landers growled as he sniffed the air. "And that goes double for the sex."

"I know." Tenkiller hung his head. "But it helps me forget."

The colonel tapped his walking stick, moving closer. "Makes the pain go away?"

"Something like that."

Tenkiller breathed in and registered Lander's scent. As a rule, angels were able to adopt an olfactory imprint—indicative of their nature and true to their divinity. The scent of cherubs was like a freshly bathed newborn. Moving to the rank and file angel, it was the aroma of honeysuckle with a trace of rose. For God's warrior angels, it was the metallic tang of honed steel employed in righteous battle. But the colonel's scent was unique, a blend of rich, hand-rubbed wood and finely tooled leather. In the heavenly hierarchy of smell, Colonel Landers was a Lamborghini rolling off the production line. Once you opened the door and breathed in, it signaled power and uniqueness.

Even though he was at the top of God's angelic hierarchy, Landers was truly humble. But, when the shit hit the fan, this heavenly handler was the go-to guy for tough situations. Because Landers had materialized into human form, Tenkiller knew the stakes were raised. There could be no more left turns for him—no detours from now on.

The fact that God had a mission for Tenkiller, the fact that the Almighty still trusted him, screamed in opposition to the fact that he had allowed people to die on his watch. God's confidence stunned him because Tenkiller felt unworthy of that trust. He was someone who'd heaped shame on the term "angel." He was someone who hid behind the bottle.

Tenkiller wanted to die and took comfort from the certain death that alcohol promised. Each day when he thought of his name, irony ripped through his gut, eviscerated his pride, and served him a steaming plate of self-loathing.

Three years ago, he had a simple assignment, watching over an extended family. The thirty-something parents had four children each from previous marriages and were content to raise their combined family in the West Texas town of Amarillo. Their youngest, Jacob, was special and the focus of Tenkiller's mission. When the young boy reached the age of twelve, he would unveil the power to heal by the laying on of hands. Jacob would be the first of the modern-day prophets, heralding the manifestation of God's eternal love.

It was Tenkiller's duty to see that the young child was protected and able to fulfill his role. But, on that hot summer night, something went wrong. The kitchen stove's valve malfunctioned, filling the home with poisonous and combustible natural gas. The parents awoke coughing and screamed for their children. Before they could rush everyone outside, the pilot light on their water heater ignited the gas. The explosion shattered windows in a two-block area and woke people miles away. All of the family died.

Jacob's guardian angel, Micah, as he was known then, figuratively died that night too. In his shame and sorrow, he took the name of Tenkiller. A name to remind him of the senseless deaths he should have prevented.

All ten of them.

Now, God wanted him, a washed-up, whoremongering, unworthy drunk to lead another mission? In the name of everything holy, he wondered why?

Landers reached out and gently took his hand. "I know your fears, son. You couldn't have saved Jacob and his family."

"That night has haunted me for three years. My spirit was in the home, and I watched over them that evening. Everything was normal. Then, I pulled my awareness away. Came back to the crib like you asked to report my progress. I left them alone, thinking they were safe. Only to let them die."

Tenkiller's shoulders shook. He put his hands to his face to hide the tears. "What happened? It never made sense."

"It was an unfortunate accident, and that's all in the past." Landers draped his arm around Tenkiller drawing him close. "Let's focus on the future because God needs you now. He knows the true measure of man, or angel, by looking at what's in the heart. I know there's a mountain of goodness within you. Ten, you have been chosen, for God loves those whom he has tested—those who still choose to do his work."

Tenkiller stood a little straighter and took a deep breath, knowing he would turn to that which was left. The one thing that would redeem him, the small spark of divinity buried within. He would nurture it to a raging fire and then rise from the flames, tempered and true. Ready to fulfill God's will.

The colonel took the angel's hand in his. "Do you have it in your heart? Do you choose to answer His call?"

In spite of Tenkiller's doubts, something fell into place. The righteous burn of resolve flooded his senses and coursed through his veins.

Landers put his lips close to the angel's ear. "Can ya do it, Ten?"

If God had confidence in Tenkiller, a sorry assed, whoring, degenerate drunk, so be it.

Then, maybe yes, he was the only one who could complete this mission. He couldn't let Landers down and certainly not God. This time things would be different.

He breathed in, and his big chest filled with pride. "I'm your man."

The handler took a step back and tapped his cane for emphasis. "Now that you're on board, we're in the beginning of the devil's takeover. Within the next few days, the devil will attempt to wreak havoc upon Earth and three more planets of the multiverse. Satan has already breached four other worlds. So, you have to convince Archer that it will be up to her and the other two sisters of the Triumvirate to stop him."

The colonel patted Ten's arm. "The situation with Archer is changing, and it's time to escalate her involvement. So, this is what I want you to do...."

18

WHAT GOES UP
MUST COME DOWN

THE ARMED GUARD IS FIVE cars away, head turning, scanning the parking lot until he reacts to the grinding of the truck's starter.

I look up from behind the steering wheel.

He runs toward me.

Two cars away, we lock eyes.

I pump the gas like crazy.

He raises his gun.

I lunge sideways.

A bullet shatters the passenger's window, sprays glass across my upper body, onto my lap. The starter keeps grinding, but the motor refuses to start—my heart thunders. Nervous sweat streaks my face.

I glance over to see him taking aim.

He draws down for another shot.

His body is erect. Both hands hold the gun steady. He exhales, and his lips curl into a predatory smile.

His eyes are deathly cold, his uniform, starched khaki.

His finger tightens on the trigger. Ten yards separate me from certain death.

Suddenly, the engine roars. I slam the truck into gear, jump the curb and duck as he fires again.

The bullet rips through my hair and punches a hole in the doorframe where my head had been a second before.

While the truck speeds forward, I peek behind and see him running toward another car on the parking lot. I gun the hot-wired vehicle across the open prairie, putting as much distance between us as possible, heading toward the Interstate's access road two miles away.

The truck's wheels bounce over the stunted sagebrush and bottom out in small, sandy depressions, causing the steering wheel to buck against my hands. I glance in the back, note that my two friends are still covered with the tarp, and confirm that the three bungee cords still hold the gurney in place.

I knew our escape would be dicey as I check the rear-view mirror. A red SUV shoots out of the parking lot, and I bite my inner cheek. With less than fifty yards between the guard and me, I ram the stick shift into third and punch the gas. A cloud of dust rises behind me as I shift into fourth. The speedometer reads sixty-five and keeps rising.

But, the more-powerful SUV surges closer.

The wind whips through the shattered passenger window, and it's decision time. Three lives and one unborn baby are now in the equation. A long, narrow ravine lies between me and the access road. I could slow down and parallel the depression until it ends, or I could catapult up a sandy incline just ahead and jump the ditch. If I do the former, the faster SUV will overtake me. If I do the latter, I have a better chance of escaping.

Even though it's risky, it's doable.

It's *Dukes of Hazard time,* but this hot-wired, beat up truck isn't the General Lee. I'm not Luke or Bo, either. But, Sheriff Roscoe P. Coltrane is hot on my trail, and unlike the fictional bad guy, the dude chasing me has a real gun, with real bullets, and a real hard-on to take my ass out.

He is getting closer. A few more seconds and I will be in

firing range. I do the math, one digit at a time. There is only one way out.

I *will* make the jump!

Tugging on my seat belt, I cinch it tight and angle the truck toward the sandy incline on the lip of the ravine. Punishing the accelerator, I whip fifteen more mph out of the old vehicle and hope it is enough.

A gunshot cracks behind me, and the back-window shatters. The red SUV is on my tail, still visible in the dust thrown up from my rear wheels. Another glance in my mirror—the guard leans out of his vehicle, aims his gun.

And then my truck hits the incline. The sudden impact slams me into the seat. My head snaps downward, and my jaw thumps against the top of my chest. Broken glass launches up from the floor, suspended in the air around me until the truck moves upward.

The glass falls to the floor.

Like a dream, two tons of American steel glide gracefully across a fifteen feet ravine—defying the law of gravity, until it lands on the other side. The front of the truck plows through the sand, ripping the barren earth like a bulldozer on steroids. The steering wheel whips from my hands, and my chest slams against the metal column.

Whiplash violates my neck muscles, my ears ring badly, and I taste blood, but thankfully, the seat belt saved me from serious injury. I lay a protective hand against my stomach and look out the broken rear window. The gurney is still in place. My two friends survived the jump.

My stolen truck rolls across the prairie. But, the guard and his SUV aren't as fortunate. The vehicle landed upside down in the middle of the ravine, wheels still spinning, steam spewing from a punched-out radiator.

Screaming in delight, I slap the steering wheel with my palm. "Take that you son-of-a-bitch!"

I put the truck in gear, a little worse for wear, but grateful to be alive.

A soft moan in back sets my hair on end. I jerk around to see Luanne Martinez's hand worm its way from under the tarp.

"Where the hell am I?" Her voice is perforated with pain. "I can't feel my fingers. And I think my freakin' arm's broken!"

19

CHAIRMAN & CEO

OFFENDER JASON BLAINE SHOOK OFF the last quiver running through his body and knew the effects of the convulsion pill had ended. The serial felon lay naked on a hospital bed, covered by a single white sheet, in a small, gray room. But, by prison standards, it was a penthouse suite. A clock on the wall read five p.m., and a plate of food sat on his bedside tray. The room's only door was closed, and according to prison protocol, a guard would be outside.

Blaine flexed his arms and met the resistance of a steel handcuff connecting his right wrist to the bed rail. Using his unfettered left hand, he snaked it down to his rectum, then forced his two dry fingers deep into his body cavity. After a moment of probing, he removed the paperclip.

This tiny piece of twisted metal was his key to freedom. The freedom promised by his new boss, along with the vow of what they would do together. From this solemn oath, the two of them would spawn more chaos, more mayhem, and more bad shit upon the chosen planets of the multiverse than he could ever imagine. Thereby putting Blaine in the epicenter, or ground zero, of mayhem, murder, and chaos.

Stan A had visited Blaine in a vision one night, two weeks ago, in his prison cell. The devil had appeared as an innocuous accountant with a deal. A deal that would free Jason Blaine and elevate him to special standing among his demons. All the felon had to do was bring death and destruction to Earth and three alternate planets.

Blaine heartily agreed that the selected worlds could use a brutal colonic irrigation, as long as he was the one inserting the tube. So, he accepted Stan's terms.

Stan wasn't forthcoming, and Blaine was savvy enough to know it. The devil didn't reveal that Blaine was expendable. Nothing more than a tool to visit destruction upon four worlds. When it was over, Blaine would be discarded or cast into the pits of eternal fire. But the felon had a hidden agenda and agreed to the devil's scheme to infiltrate Hell and usurp Stan. Then Blaine would become the next Chairman and CEO of Lost Souls, Inc.

Blaine ended his rumination and wiped the paperclip on the bedsheet. He pressed the tip against the steel bed rail until it formed a ninety-degree bend with a quarter-inch tip. Close enough to resemble the tooth of a real handcuff key.

But, a noise in the hallway caused Blaine to pause. Voices drifted through his door. The male guard outside laughed. A female, probably a nurse, joined in, then asked, "Are you guarding 'The Priest?'"

"The one and only." The offender heard the officer scoot his chair on the linoleum floor, scraping the metal leg tips against the surface.

"I read about him in the paper." The nurse's voice rose in apprehension. "Didn't he terrorize some woman?"

"Yeah, and the press dubbed him 'The Priest' because that sick bastard had a garage with a real Catholic confessional inside. Kept her chained in it for thirteen days—with only a bucket for her eliminations. He gave her plenty of food and water and didn't touch a hair on her head. But after what he did to her, she'd have been better off dead."

"What'd he do?" The female's voice was husky, mining the edge of fearful interest.

Jason Blaine went rock hard at the memory.

There was a pause before the guard responded, "During his trial, the scumbag said he just talked to her. Hours on end for thirteen days."

"Did Blaine know her?"

"By all accounts, he picked her on impulse."

"So, if he didn't physically hurt her, what happened?"

"There weren't no physical proof." The officer coughed. "But Blaine must have got into her head. The prosecutor made that assumption, too. With thirteen days, he had plenty of time to peel back the layers of her mind, one by one, like removing extra winter clothing. Until he reached the bare core of her soul."

"Did she testify against him?"

"No. She was at the trial, but then, she wasn't there. Her eyes were vacant. The light inside was gone. Whatever that asshole did, he sucked out everything that made her human and left an empty shell."

"Dear God."

The guard continued, "But she did react after Blaine was found guilty."

"Did he say something?"

"As they drug him out of the court, he leaned toward her. That piece of Nazi trash puffed up, looked her in the eye and said, 'My gift is the rotting rose that molders upon your mother's corpse, and if you ever awake from your nightmare, remember what I've done to you.'"

"Whatever his message meant, she screamed. Screamed like the demons of Hell were after her. And I guess they were. She couldn't stop until she collapsed at the prosecutor's feet. I was there," the guard's voice cracked. "People inside the courtroom gasped. The room erupted into a panic."

"Is she all right? Where is she now?"

"Her future don't look too good. She's at the Big Spring State Hospital. They say she just sits there and holds herself, rocking back and forth." The guard cleared his throat. "That sumbitch is pure evil. I work on his pod at the prison and lemme tell you, he's got a way of getting inside your mind. Knowing stuff. All kinds of weird things. Things you don't want no one to know. It's like he's got a psychic pipeline that sucks out your darkest shit and then puts a wicked twist on it. Throws it back in your face. I seen him do it to other officers, and he done it to me. And I swear that's what he did to the poor woman."

"The Priest and his confessional." Pity and disgust filled her voice.

"Never laid a finger on her," the officer added. "But he done raped her mind."

The nurse went silent, then whispered, "Have you checked on him? Are we safe?"

"Thirty minutes ago I looked in on the jerkin' jitterbug. He was still shaking like a Baptist sinner at a tent revival. Don't expect much trouble from that lowlife."

Jason Blaine twisted the bent paperclip in the keyhole and popped the handcuff off his right wrist. Satan's new henchman formed a fist and acknowledged two things. First, the guard had a big mouth, and, second, his jailer's life was going to turn to shit.

Real fast.

20

THE RIVER RUNS SWIFT AND DEEP

JASON BLAINE GLANCED UP AT his hospital room's wall clock and remembered the timeline Stan had given him in his vision. The devil, who was psychically in tune with the future, had revealed that the prison guard would enter Blaine's hospital room at exactly 5:35 p.m. Four minutes later, the jailhouse sentry would be dead, stripped and lying in Blaine's bed.

At precisely 6:35, a curious nurse would notice the guard's absence and sound the alarm.

It would be 6:45 before the police arrived.

When the clock marked 6:46, Amarillo PD Officer Justin League would open offender Blaine's door, with gun drawn, and discover the dead correctional officer.

The devil further stated that while the police were processing the crime scene, Jason Blaine would be dining at Stan's remote countryside home, savoring a pint of Guinness and his first steak since he had entered prison one year ago. Later, he and Stan A would smoke their H. Upmann cigars while sipping a rare 1787 Chateau Lafite.

Undoubtedly it would be the world's most expensive wine.

Blaine closed his eyes and thought of events that had led him here. Primarily, his father, the ruthless psychopath who had molded Blaine's life. A man who had versed him in the nuances of sophisticated living, as well as Neo-Nazi doctrine. A man who had unleashed a river of darkness within his malleable son.

Blaine opened his eyes. The room's clock now read 5:35, and the door opened. The guard slowly approached Blaine's bed with his hand on his gun.

Four minutes later, the jailer was dead from a crushed windpipe. And five minutes after that, Jason Blaine sauntered out the front hospital exit. Dressed in the guard's clothes, he pulled his hat brim down and passed under the CCTV. Blaine was on his way to an important dinner date.

He ducked around the corner and was greeted by a suited chauffeur who bowed slightly and opened the side door of a black stretch limousine. He glanced at the dead man's wristwatch and tapped the crystal.

Blaine's world was always on time.

And the river, swift and deep, ran its course.

21

HOPE & DESPAIR

HOPE STOOD NAKED IN FRONT of her bathroom mirror and stared at what should have been an attractive, young woman's body. But blotchy patches of cancer streaked her torso, and her once black hair was completely white. She had aged internally in the past month and felt the erratic pulse of her diseased heart. If prior experience were any indicator, within a few days, both kidneys would fail.

She looked at the peeling paint on the wall of her tiny apartment bathroom and picked at the scabs on her arm until something moved inside her chest, something she didn't want to consider, something not good.

To abort her morbid thoughts, she focused upon the tattoos on the back of each hand. Four letters sprawled daintily across her left spelled *Hope,* in strokes both airy and feminine. The name *Despair* raged in angry cursive on the right.

Hope was an extreme medical empath with the disconcerting ability to link, deeply, intimately, with other human beings. If she smelled someone's scent, touched their skin, or connected through her other senses, she formed a psychic connection and absorbed the negative energy of any illness in their body. After numerous healings, the malignant force had to be purged from Hope, or she would develop and die from the same diseases.

Even though her gift compelled her to heal those she was drawn to, she had to limit her contact with the rest of humanity.

She reached for a vial of Mentholatum on the bathroom counter. At the age of twenty-two, she shouldn't have deformed arthritic hands, but because of a recent healing, she now did. Even the act of unscrewing the lid was hellishly painful. Placing a small amount of the ointment in each nostril, she breathed in, relishing the icy, biting sensation that told her it was working. Working well enough to block the scent of humans and avoid a psychic connection if they got too close.

Putting the vial back on the cracked countertop, she reached for the Oakley wraparound sunglasses. The lens of which had been sanded to obscure her sight and hamper a paranormal coupling via her eyes.

She plunged a Sennheiser earbud deep into each ear canal, relying on the manufacturer's promise of three levels of noise reduction. But, to achieve total sound blockage, Hope started the first tune in a three hundred song library of ragged, head-banging, ear-popping music, thereby employing another strategy to discourage an empathic union from verbal intercourse.

Hope pushed her arthritic hands into a pair of black, stretch gloves, shrugged into a long-sleeved shirt, and tugged on heavy cotton pants. She pulled on hiking boots, then adjusted her black hoodie so that it covered her white, spiked hair. Another strategy to limit accidental skin contact with people.

Because of her peculiar gift, she had long ago given up hugs from family or friends, said no to parties and gatherings, and become a social recluse who shunned physical contact.

Shunned it out of self-preservation.

But her life balanced upon a razor's edge. There was a limit to the amount of absorbed illness she could retain.

Every sixth day, Hope insulated her senses with sunglasses, hoodie, earbuds, and Mentholatum and followed her internal

GPS to the next person to heal. And, in the process of using her divine gift, she rode ever closer to death by absorbing each subject's disease.

But, there was a price to pay, and a viperous bill lay upon Hope's desk. For her to continue living, all of the absorbed suffering, all of the malaise and illness built up within her had to be purged. And that is when her alternate personality emerged.

Hope fisted her twisted hands. Her savior's name, tattooed on her flesh under the right glove, was Despair.

She looked at her image in the mirror, hoodie pulled down, exposed flesh covered, and she inhaled. Enjoyed the harsh bite of Mentholatum in her nostrils. Relished the music in her ears. Welcomed the sanded shades and embraced the protection of her clothes. But, what she needed was the life-saving relief of a negative energy purge. A psychic enema administered by her alter ego, Despair.

Unless he took over, and soon, she was totally screwed. The pain and misery from multiple inflictions pulsed inside her fragile body, affecting her organs and blistering her flesh with pus-filled ulcers.

In a few days, Despair would emerge and clear all the negative energy she had drawn from the ones she'd healed. But, there was a catch. The recipient of the malignant force Despair would drain from her body had to have a heart and soul without redeeming qualities. Had to be a person whose actions and thoughts lived in the darkest region of Hell. And, to save Hope's life, the receptacle had to agree to a personal death sentence.

If no one accepted, Hope would be forced to mount and ride the hellish creature called Darkness past the valley of hope into the plains of death.

Which wasn't high on her bucket list, either.

22

NO SHIRT, NO SHOES,
YOU STILL GET SERVICE

I STOMP THE TRUCK'S ACCELERATOR and blast down Interstate 40, ripping past Amarillo businesses—fast-food chains, convenience stores, and strip malls. Wind rushes through two bullet-shattered windows and swirls trash across the floor of the hot-wired Ford.

A glance over my shoulder—both friends are still strapped to their gurney and in need of a doctor.

Luanne is conscious and waves her hand. I shout over the wind noise. "Luanne, is Jacqui awake?"

"I've been shaking her. She's not responding."

"Is she breathing?"

Luanne pulls the tarp down and shakes her head. "I can't tell. If she is, it's really shallow."

This could be a reaction to her sedation at Stan's farm.

"Hang on. I'll get you both to a doctor."

The evening rush hour traffic is hellacious, and I swerve in and out of the lanes. The hospital district is miles away, and I'm watching for a closer emergency clinic—anything with a doctor.

Careening through the congested, aggressive traffic, I get several angry horn blasts and a few clenched fists.

I don't give a damn whether they like my driving or not. Scanning the billboards, I see one up ahead that advertises quick medical attention. In one-half mile, I accelerate down the exit ramp and angle across the access road traffic. A quick tap on my brakes and a right turn brings me to the emergency clinic's reception door.

I lean on the vehicle's horn, and a nurse rushes through the sliding glass entrance, gives me a once over, and glances in the truck's bed.

I jump out, drop the tailgate, unhook the bungee cords. Then we both remove the gurney.

The nurse discards the tarp covering my two friends and isn't fazed with their nudity. Her face screams crisis mode—alert eyes acknowledge the conscious Luanne, then move to the immobile Jacqui.

A quick assessment of vital signs produces a frown. "She's not breathing and has a faint pulse." The RN tips Jacqui's head back and puts a mouth to mouth resuscitation device in place. In between rescue breaths, she motions me to roll the trolley inside.

I shove the cart through the sliding doors and sprint down the hall into the clinic's emergency room. Two assistants are waiting inside. One attaches electrodes then wraps a blood pressure cuff around Jacqui's upper arm. Another helps the nude Luanne off the trolley, checks her arm, then hands her a pair of hospital scrubs.

I stare at the vital sign's monitor, praying for a miracle. A few years ago, in my home dimension, on Earth, I entered Allen Costas's psychic enhancement program and met Jacqui and Luanne. The other participants were standoffish and distant. But not these two girls. They extended their hand and welcomed me into their hearts. Seeing their acceptance of me thawed the rest of the students, and I quickly became their confidant and friend.

I freely give Jacqui and Luanne my unconditional support and love. Unfortunately, Jacqui's heartbeat is sporadic and without a regular rhythm. The nurse glances up. Assesses the situation. The heartbeat flatlines. The RN starts CPR and after several rounds shakes her head in frustration.

A moment of quiet, then the team explodes into action.

The crash cart is thrust forward and opened. A manual heart defibrillator removed.

The two paddles are jelled up, rubbed against each other, and placed on Jacqui's bare chest.

Dials are set. A whine, and then a short beep signals discharge state. The nurse glances at the vital sign's monitor. *"Clear!"*

Jacqui's torso lurches upward from the electrical charge. Everyone looks at the screen.

Nothing.

Not a pulse. Not a blip on the display. Not a damn thing.

The defibrillator recharges. The nurse tries again.

And again.

"Goddammit!" I slam my fist into the wall. Disbelief twists my soul. In the space of thirty minutes, I'd given everything I had to rescue my two friends. But that wasn't enough for Jacqui. If I can't save her, then how in the hell can I be expected to prevent destruction upon four worlds?

23

ONE PUMP OR TWO?

SAFELY ENSCONCED BEHIND HIS BOLTED office door, Dr. Ron Smith tested the limits of his double-wide executive chair with three hundred pounds of Funyuns enhanced bulk—layered over a five-foot frame. The fact that he was almost as wide as he was tall never bothered him. However, the cost of replacing his desk chair every few months did.

Sterile fluorescent light banished the darkness in his windowless, trophy room. Off limits to his three-medical staff, the doctor's upscale office hid a display of one hundred pairs of used shoes. His purloined footwear was exhibited on four bookshelves, artfully arranged across the floor, and proudly displayed on his desk. Every square inch of space here held a secret he'd hidden from the public since he hit puberty. Today's world was littered by those coming out of the closet. But he'd never do that because the act of doing something secretive and taboo added a forbidden thrill to his footwear obsession.

He leaned toward his desk, stuck his nose deep inside a lady's size seven hightop, and inhaled. Like taking a nose hit off a joint, he sucked in the tart and tangy odor, holding it in until his eyes lost focus and his head spun. Smith collapsed back in his chair and knew he was a sick man. A hundred stolen shoes attested to the fact that he was—very sick.

Deliciously. Deliriously. Sick.

The misfit medico owned this small emergency clinic and catered to the affluent crowd—a crowd who detested long waits to see a doctor and would pay extra for prompt attention.

But, it was the emergency room traffic that fueled his fetish. When an injured, female patient arrived, out came the scissors. Off came the clothes. Shoes were carefully unlaced, removed, and sealed inside a plastic bag. The accident victim would be patched together and discharged in a semi-sedated state. Inevitably, the patient's shoes missed the trip home, leaving Dr. Smith with another trophy for his beloved collection.

Anything that carried the owner's scent was fair game. Smith ran his fingers down the hightop's tongue, across the eyelets, tugging its white laces. He glanced up at his collection of stolen and sweaty and smelly footwear. His eyes visually caressed sandals, slippers, running shoes, yoga shoes, and tennis shoes. This was a thriving, robust collection, rounded out with Mary Janes, platforms, flip-flops, high heels, and pumps.

Last week's additions included a pair of clogs, knee-high moccasins, vintage Jelly shoes—all of which promised endless hours of stimulation.

His intercom buzzed. Dr. Smith straightened up. The chair screeched in protest.

"Emergency room has two admissions."

"Prep the patients. I'm on the way."

Stepping out of his secretive shoe-a-rama, Dr. Smith locked the door behind him and hoped for something interesting. Not a medical challenge with his next two patients. No, he was desperate for a pair of seven-inch Jimmy Choo stilettos—something to put a little more sin in his scintillating collection.

24

HELL ON WHEELS

HOPE GRIPPED THE BUMPER OF a speeding UPS truck, drafting behind it at seventy mph on her customized electric skateboard. Strip malls, nail salons, and bank branches zipped by on either side of the Interstate as she followed her intuitive sense.

She preferred hitching a ride behind large trucks because her board's lithium batteries only provided fifteen minutes of highway speed or one-half hour at a slower pace. She glanced down at the road and realized the possibility of falling and being shredded by the asphalt wasn't as big a concern as being flattened by the eighty-thousand-pound semis around her.

Whether Hope was ready for it or not, today was trash day. Once a week for the past five years, she was driven by an overpowering urge to seek out and absorb an unknown illness from the critically ill, ultimately saving someone's life. The unsuspecting subject was always on death's door or just a whimper inside it.

Like the trash trucks that picked up refuse until they were full, Hope also had her limit. Last week, she had done an unexpected double pickup from Siamese twins with liver failure and would be punishing her physical health with this load today.

The urge to purge couldn't occur soon enough—hopefully before her subject's diseases consumed her. Hope had no control over this strange process. Being led by an internal signal, she heeded her strange spiritual gift. A gift inherited from her mother's side, handed down to the females for the past five generations.

God gave her an ability she never asked for. Yet, she faithfully performed her duties, realizing she was part of a larger plan. She learned the Creator awarded His loyal soldiers as they manifested His will. Hope had faithfully fulfilled her duties, line upon line, here a little, there a little, action by action. Then, in confirmation, a glimmer of spiritual insight settled softly in her mind.

The still, small voice from within prickled the nape of her neck. "The one you save today is flanked by her two friends, who complete the Triumvirate of Sisters. This unlikely band of souls, along with a fallen angel, and yourself, will either join forces with or oppose the devil and his plans. Choose thou, thy path."

Hope released her grip on the truck's bumper when her internal compass signaled a change of direction. She balanced on the skateboard, looked over her sanded-out sunglass's lenses, and engaged the high-speed electric motor with her right heel.

Choose thou, thy path. The words resonated inside her. She would rise to the challenge, completing the spiritual obligation started five generations ago. Her path was one of goodness and light, so damn the devil and his minions.

Moving with the traffic, Hope angled across the Interstate onto the access road. She refrained from giving the middle-finger to the moronic motorists who honked at her. Fortunately, the skateboard kept her ahead of the traffic, and she coasted into an emergency care clinic driveway.

Standing on the pavement, she kicked down on the tail of the skateboard, caught the opposite end in her hand as it popped up, then propped it against the facility's outside wall.

Animal quiet, she padded down the hall, led by her spiritual GPS into the emergency room.

DR. RON SMITH TOOK A final, wistful look inside his secretive shoe-a-topia before locking the door. With high hopes for a special acquisition, he started down the hallway—steps away from possibly acquiring some sinful Jimmy Choo's. Seductive, seven-inch stilettos. Sexy, patent leather, Jimmy Choos.

He turned into the ER and noticed the patient.

Flatlined. Correct.

Female. Correct.

Nude. Correct.

No shoes. *Shit!*

His ruptured dream played a death dirge for his dark fantasy. A fantasy now on the edge of Choo-a-cide. Seconds later, his attention moved to his technicians and nurse who were transfixed, with mouths open. They watched a small, young woman, clothed from head to toes, remove her gloves and approach the flat-lined patient. Two other females, possibly friends of the dead victim, were stunned by the odd intrusion.

The doctor opened his mouth to speak until the pixie-like female placed both palms upon the deceased patient's chest. A star-bright burst of light came from her hands, and the doctor's pupils contracted from the intensity. The light bathed everyone in the room Sucked the breath from their lungs. Bled the darkness from their souls.

The dead woman breathed in. Her body surged upward, and her vital signs ignited across the monitor.

THE MOMENT SHE TOUCHED THE deceased woman's chest,

personal information and images cycled through Hope's mind. Pictures of a facility where hundreds of unfortunate souls were being drained of their lifeblood. A structure where evil thrived at the cost of human life. A building hiding unspeakable horror. A place the devil called home.

Hope intuitively knew everything about Jacqui and siphoned her pain and suffering, as well as the medical complications from her earlier sedation. In a profound statement that God still cares, Hope released her from death. When she removed her hands from Jacqui's chest, the healer staggered backward.

DR. SMITH REELED FROM THE blinding white light. Absorbing a frontal impact of God's sacred power, he also spiritually mainlined the essence of love and rejuvenation. In the space of seconds, he knew that he was still the same, yet everything had changed. The young woman who had ignited the celestial light turned from the patient she'd healed and stumbled toward him.

Falling into his arms, her ungloved hands touched his bare forearms, and the doctor screamed, even though no sound left his lips. A brilliant supernova explosion burst inside his mind, a light that laid bare all his sins, his misguided thoughts, his hidden secrets.

His body shook. His mind trembled. For the first time in decades, he was whole again.

The young healer gasped, released his arms, and leaned toward his ear. "God just gave you a second chance. Don't fuck it up!"

HOPE REGAINED HER EQUILIBRIUM, PUT her gloves back on, and left her audience stunned and shellacked, silent and shocked. The sound of Jacqui's vital signs followed her and faded away as she exited the facility and mounted her skateboard. Once on the access road, she noticed the thrift store at the top of the hill. She engaged the high-speed electric motor just as her stomach curled in a sensual knot. Bitten by the lust bug, Hope's only cure was some bitchin', seven-inch stilettos. Preferably gently used Jimmy Choos.

THE RAP, RAP, RAPTOR

ONE YEAR AGO, A CORRECTIONAL officer who called himself the Raptor cut a deal with offender Jason Blaine. The Cretaceous reptile wanted cocaine—a lot of it. Like his namesake, the Raptor was a scavenger and promised to supply the Neo-Nazi with foraged prison intelligence, the identities of High-Security informants, and the times for contraband shakedowns.

If the information existed, the Raptor was privy to it. That was why Jason Blaine parked with his new boss, Stan, on the side of a desolate county road, fifteen miles from the Amarillo prison. According to the Raptor, a special chain bus, transporting thirty of the worst offenders in the Texas penal system, would pass by their hidden spot on the way to the maximum security facility in Amarillo.

Most, if not all, were known by Blaine and had been involved in his criminal empire during the past twenty years. This was a platoon spawned in Hell because Stan needed the manpower to bring destruction to four more worlds. The devil was certain this busload of psychopaths could do it.

Sitting in his parked limo off the main road, Stan cranked up the AC and reached into the bag of Cheetos between his thighs. He fished out a handful of the crunchy, cheesy junk food, popped several in his mouth, then glanced out the driver's window.

Stan licked orange crumbs off his fingers. "Looks like the chain bus is on time."

BLAINE CASUALLY GLANCED OVER HIS shoulder, then opened the sedan's door and slithered out. The bus was a mile away and descending into a low depression. When it was out of sight, he picked up two tire-puncturing spike strips and spread them over both lanes. Since there was a deep drop-off on either side of the pavement, the bus would either stop or run over the sharpened spikes. To ensure the driver ran over them before he saw them, Blaine deployed the strips ten yards on the downward side of the hill.

Once the tires blew, the guards would be like two bass in a barrel. Knowing the officers only had metal batons and bare knuckles, Blaine stacked the odds in his favor by bringing a gun to a potential fistfight. His extraction tool for the two fish was an AK-47 assault rifle with a seventy-five round drum magazine. In Blaine's world, violent overkill was a fact of life and invariably decided who lived and who died.

The Neo-Nazi hid behind a large cottonwood tree near the road and gripped the stock of his weapon. It was time to kick some ass.

FOR OFFICER DANIELS, THE NOISE from the whining offenders was deafening. Behind his driver's seat, the prison Bluebird had two rows of fifteen seats. With an offender chained to each one, that totaled thirty sweaty, smelly, psycho shit heads. All the windows were down to ventilate the stench of confined bodies, yet all it did was swirl the smell into a tart, invisible armpit that hung in the air.

Daniels, one hand on the wheel, removed his hat and wiped sweat from his brow. He nodded to his partner, Collins, who stood in the stairwell, next to the door. The Bluebird didn't have AC, and the outside temperature was 107 degrees, hot enough to put the sizzle in a steak.

Behind the driver's seat, a small barred door separated the officers from the felons. Felons who were handcuffed and wore leg shackles, which kept them from moving anything, except their damn mouths.

As the vehicle sped up the hill, the heated, outside air rushed over the window bars, creating a shrill howl that eviscerated the manic noise of the unruly criminals.

When Daniels crested the top of the hill, he looked ahead and recognized the spike strips across both sides of the road. Instinctively, he jerked the wheel to the right. "Hang on Collins." With no way to avoid the sharpened prongs, Daniels let off the gas and steadied the wheel as all the tires blew.

Silence filled the bus as thirty criminals realized something monumental was happening. They looked around and began cheering a man running toward the wingless Bluebird. His face twisted with feral intensity, and he carried a bad-ass piece of artillery like he knew how to use it.

OFFICER COLLINS REACHED DOWN TO his ankle holster and removed a smuggled .38 caliber revolver. He looked at Daniels and grinned. "When I give the word, open the door. I've got vermin to shoot."

JASON BLAINE KEPT HIS EYES ON the bus door as he pounded across the pavement. His feet slapped the road, and he leveled the AK-47 at the driver's cabin. Some of the offenders inside the bus recognized him and shrieked in joy while flashing gang signs. For just a second, Blaine stared into their faces and smiled, a smile that ruptured into surprise when he tripped on a piece of a blown-out tire. He stumbled to the ground, dropped the rifle, and shredded his hands on the pavement. The gun skittered across the road.

Blaine started to get up, but the bus door opened, and a correctional officer jumped to the ground. Assuming a shooter's stance, the guard was fifteen feet away and pointed his revolver at Blaine's torso.

"WELL, IF IT AIN'T THE big, bad offender." Officer Collins motioned with his gun for Blaine to stand and back away from the AK-47.

The guard sighted down the barrel. "Go for it, shithead. If you got the balls, give it a try."

Blaine put his hands to his head.

"What time you got, offender?"

Blaine shrugged.

"You got my dead brother's watch on your right wrist. The guard you murdered when you escaped from the hospital."

"You're here to avenge his death?"

"Might look at it that way. When I heard that some of your crew were transferring to Amarillo, I volunteered for the trip, hoping I might run into you. Took a big chance on smuggling this piece aboard the Bluebird, but it looks like I won the lottery."

Collins motioned with his gun. "Go ahead. I'll give you a two-second start for the AK before I shoot. That's more than you did for my brother."

Blaine lowered his hands. "So, what? This will look like self-defense?"

"Something like that."

"It doesn't have to go like this, Boss. There's always room in my organization for someone with your initiative."

"Thought you might wimp out. So, fuck your head start."

Collins tightened his finger on the trigger.

The offender smiled and opened his arms. "You just lost the race, pig."

DANIELS STOOD BEHIND COLLINS AND using both hands, swung a two-foot metal baton. Hard. A whistling sound cut the air as rigid metal met Collins's face. Met it with a vengeance and dropped him hard.

Thirty felons cheered. Daniels turned toward the bus, bowed, then wiped the blood from his baton. He clapped Blaine upon the back.

BLAINE MOPPED THE SWEAT FROM his face and motioned to Stan in the idling limo. In Blaine's world, everything was on time. He looked at the dead guard's watch, flicking imaginary lint off the dial. Then he put his arm around the rogue officer's shoulders and pointed to a blacked-out tour bus he had parked down the road earlier. "Release my friends inside the Bluebird, and then you can drive us to our new home."

Jason Blaine took a Ziplock baggie of coke from his pocket and flipped it to the officer. "Good work, Raptor."

26

TOUCHED BY THE LIGHT

I THINK THE EMERGENCY CLINIC doctor was a bit touched by the light because he didn't ask us any questions. Like, why were the two girls nude? Where did the bullet holes in the truck come from? Who was the mystery woman that brought Jacqui Chen back to life?

Somehow, we got out of the trauma center without having to answer a single inquiry. When I offered to pay, the doctor refused, said this was the best thing that had ever happened to him. Even better than Jimmy Choos. Whatever the hell *that* means.

On the wild ride from Stan's farm, Luanne thought her arm broke after the pickup launched across the ravine, but it turned out that the bungee cord holding her in place had pinched a nerve, causing severe pain. Even though my friends were bled at the farm, the doctor checked the two girls over and found them to be amazingly healthy.

On the way home, I stopped at Target and bought them new clothes so that they could shed the medical scrubs they got at the clinic. The three of us are back at my parents' house and sit on the living room couch. I'm next to the end table with the laptop. Luanne is to my right, and Jacqui is on the far end.

I brief them on the female triumvirate, or Sisters of Three, as well as Tenkiller and Stan A's plan to bring destruction into four more planets of the multiverse.

Jacqui Chen flips her long, black hair back and thumps her thigh with her fist. "What makes the three of us able to save the worlds?"

"Yeah." Luanne leans forward, blinking her large brown eyes. "How come we're so special?"

"I don't know. This is bizarre, even to me." I turn my laptop on and adjust the screen. "So, what's your intuition say?"

My two friends exchange glances.

Luanne punches me on the arm. "My sixth sense's screaming, run, run, run like a mother on this one. But, I'm feeling bored now, so let's do it."

Leaning forward, I look at Jacqui. "What're you thinking?"

"Archer, I've beaten death once today, and I'm ready to spit in the devil's eye. Come hell or high water, I'm in, too."

My laptop's news app cuts in and spews out an emergency update. "This breaking news, an anonymous tip led officers to a facility where hundreds of sedated victims were being bled to death. The purpose of the blood collection is not clear. Stay tuned, and we will keep you posted as developments occur."

Luanne tips an imaginary hat. "Congo rats." She winks her eye. "That's millennial speak for cong-rat-ulations, Archer. It's amazing what your phone call to the police did." Both girls give me a high five.

I glance at the laptop's screen and watch the live coverage of the blood farm fade to static. Probably technical difficulties with the feed, so I gather my thoughts on how to stop Stan.

A cool sensation runs across my shoulder, and Luanne puts her hand to her mouth. "Archer, look. The freakin' laptop."

I turn and take a quick breath. A cold, grey fog gushes out of the computer screen. It's not on fire, and I don't smell smoke. "What the hell is this?"

The dense haze flows across the top of the couch and covers the three of us from neck to toe.

I need to move and don't have the power. I need to scream and don't have a voice. I need to get it together and don't have a place to start.

I can't do shit. This scenario has gone from what the hell is happening. To a screaming, *OhmyGodohmyGodohmyGod!*

After a glance, I see Stan's scabby hand emerge from inside the laptop's screen and pass through the monitor toward my face. The creep factor multiplies itself to twice the square root of weird, then spikes to the umpteenth power of unnatural. This whole mess delivers a double-tap to my mind.

There must be a paralytic agent in the fog because my body's freeze-dried and plastered in place. Inches from my face, the blistered, abraded fingers open wide. The center of the palm reveals a set of human lips that pull back—exposing needle-honed teeth that glisten with bloody saliva. Teeth that extend deep into the oral cavity.

I look over at my two friends. Their bodies are perfectly still, heads bowed, and they're out for the count. Stan's hand is still coming through the laptop screen, extending toward me until his fingers touch my cheeks, tighten against my skin, and clamp the sides of my face. They are pulling me so close that my lips nearly touch the palm's lips. When flesh meets flesh, I taste the overpowering flavor of Cheetos and smell the rotting remnants of a recent meal.

Then, my world goes black.

27

SWEET DREAMS BABY

IN THIS STAN-ORCHESTRATED FORCED memory, I'm stand-ing in front of the entrance to Costas's psychic espionage facility and about to relive killing my parents. The devil has unlocked my mind to replay this devastating loss, and I'm powerless to stop the process.

It's like I'm watching a movie of myself peering through the facility's glass door and see Mom and Dad lying on separate hospital beds. Both are unconscious and oblivious to the activity around them. Inside the spacious room six white-coated technicians are on the floor, two of which tend to my parents and an additional one who monitors the security console. That makes seven people. Before I escaped from my cell fifteen minutes ago, on the way to rescue my parents, Mom's image appeared on the TV monitor, and she told me that she could control five people. This is two more than she can handle.

A closed-circuit television screen is just above the security console, and even though Mom is unconscious, her subconscious can project her image on the TV. When it flashes on, she beacons me to move. The door's electronic lock retracts, and I push my way inside.

No one notices me at first. People move and talk, check charts, and go about their duties. One technician looks my way, raises his hand, but before he can sound an alarm, the man's body movements cease, his arms go limp. The worker's face still reflects alarm over my presence as Mom takes over. Silence fills the room as the other attendants freeze in place.

I weave around the immobile technicians, careful not to touch them or look in their eyes.

Mom maintains control of the room, and I plant myself next to her bed. But a jerky movement from the corner of my eye startles me. A lone technician moves toward me like a marionette. His awkward movements show his attempt to fight against Mother's mental control.

A glance at the flat screen. Mom's demeanor says that she can handle this. Reassured, I notice the tray in the man's hands. It holds two ampoules of amber liquid and a couple of syringes.

On TV, Mom nods her head at me. "Archer, I had him compound the drug that will awaken us from our permanent dimensional induction trance. Empty one vial in each of our IV ports."

The puppet stops in front of me, and his harsh breath washes across my face. He fights against Mom's control—spittle flies from his mouth and runs down his lower lip. His eyes jerk from side to side, and I avoid looking at him when I pick up a vial and one syringe.

I remove the syringe's protective wrapper, pop the cap off, and insert the needle in the bottle's rubber stopper. Then I turn it up, pull the plunger back, and fill the hypodermic. In the back of my mind, I listen to the steady electronic heartbeats coming from my parents' vital sign's monitors.

Within a few minutes, I deliver both doses into their bloodstream. Mom's image is still on the closed-circuit television, and the immobile technicians are as frozen as Mount Rushmore. Still, something bothers me.

My feeling of dread surges when the man who brings the vials jerks and drops his tray. The empty glass ampoules shatter on the floor. A nearby worker twists around to face me. His companion, at Dad's side, also begins to move.

I scan the room and see the emerging scowls on several faces. And then I hear a door crash open. Le Cadavre rushes in, past the security console, with three armed thugs behind him.

"Mom, I need some help. *Now.*"

A quick look at the TV screen stuns me to the core. What the hell is going on? Mom's face is now lifeless. Her mouth slack. Yet, there is a glimmer of recognition in her eyes. I know she can still hear me.

Le Cadavre boldly approaches. Glares at me. Rumbles with laughter. "You see, Archer, your mother isn't the only one with psychic ability. I knew what she was planning before she had the technician make the compound. So, I switched her wake-up drug with a recipe of my own. A batch of nasty chemicals that brings death in minutes." He glances at his watch. "By the looks of it, it's sixty seconds till eternity."

I square off with him. "You're lying."

"If I am," he spreads his hands, "why can't your mother control me?"

I scan the room, and my heart thumps up my throat. The once immobile technicians begin to circle me. Some jerk like zombies, others are more coordinated.

Le Cadavre cups his hand behind his ear. "Listen, what's that sound?"

What the hell is he talking about? I look around, frantic to understand. Then, I hear it—the unmistakable sound of my parents' telemetry. The frantic pinging of two vital sign's monitors. It is the signal of impending death. My parents' hearts are beating way too fast.

I glance at Mom's monitor. Her pulse registers one hundred thirty-five. Dad's is over one forty.

Both are climbing.

The two machines emit a warning signal.

He grins. "How does it feel, Archer, knowing that your parents are alive, after a staged death, only to be killed by you?"

I don't have time to think. Eleven men surround me. Like a lone kid, circled by thugs, I face off with insurmountable odds. Odds that tell me I am so screwed.

"Feel all alone, Archer?" Le Cadavre smirks. "Such a pity. But know when your mother and father are dead, there'll be someone you can lean on, and that's me."

I have no idea what he is talking about. My focus is on my parents. Mom's television image draws my attention. There is something strange in her eyes.

I look back at Le Cadavre. "What the hell are you talking about, asshole?"

He nods his head. "Thirty seconds, Archer. Don't interrupt me because I have some news for you." He points to Mother's flat-screen image. "Just keep your eyes on her."

All I can focus on is the raging rhythm of my parents' heartbeats.

Le Cadavre taps his watch. "It was a late night in the summer of 1994 when I first met your mother. She was on her way home when I overpowered her and took what I wanted. She begged me to stop, but I didn't until I had my fill. The police weren't involved, and your father never learned of your mother's little secret. A secret that grew for nine months. She prayed that it was your father's child, but in her heart, she knew better."

Shame twists Mom's face.

My mouth goes dry. My heart hammers a hole in my chest. My stomach churns with dread.

Mom's eyes are alive with abject fear. The fear generated by the truth.

"Fifteen seconds and counting, Archer."

The vital signs warning shrills again.

My pulse throbs in my temple. "You're making this shit up."

"Could be, Archer, but the proof is in the pudding." He

lifts his shirt to expose a small, tan birthmark in the shape of a crescent.

My throat closes shut, barely stifling my scream.

"Ever see this, Archer? You have one in the same place. I saw it before I Tazed you at the ranch house. Then I remembered that night when I showed your mother what a real man was like."

My hands shake as I slowly lift my scrub top. I glance down. There is an identical mark, just like his.

"This can't be true." But, when I look in Mother's eyes, I know it is.

Le Cadavre sees it, too.

Both vital signs monitors shriek a final, fatal warning—Mother and Father flat line.

In the space of five minutes, I realize three things. We can't escape, I have killed both my parents, and the monster called Le Cadavre is my real father!

He holds his arms out. "You're not alone while I'm here, Archer." He puckers his lips and beckons me closer. "Come give Daddy a kiss."

I pull away from the devil's orchestrated memory and remember later exposing Le Cadavre's lie. In his world, he layers degrees of truth within lies. Which doesn't totally negate him from being my father. It just lessens the possibility.

The emotional weight of killing my parents leaves me trembling from internal fury. A wracking sob shakes my body. I'm trapped between the razor edges of unbearable rage and agonizing grief. Terror extends its fangs, rips my heart apart, slices my sanity, and devours my soul.

How dare Stan screw with my mind and make me relive all the horror and guilt from my recent past. In a moment of mental clarity, I wonder, is there a method to his madness, and what does it mean?

28

GUILTY AS CHARGED

THE GILDED EDGE OF CONSCIOUSNESS slices the horrible recollection of my parenticide away. I'm lightheaded yet able to move, so I shift on the couch and shake Luanne Martinez's shoulder. "Hey, you all right?"

She lifts her head, glassy-eyed yet awake. "I just had a horrible memory."

Jacqui Chen, who is next to Luanne, looks groggy. "What the hell! I just relived the worst day of my life. What's going on?"

Both friends stare at me, and guilt ripples through my gut. Putting my mind in drive, I plow ahead with my painful recollection and explain how I killed my parents.

Luanne puts her arm around my shoulder. "Archer, you didn't kill them. Le Cadavre did by substituting the poison."

Jacqui reaches across Luanne and pats my leg. "You were set up. Don't blame yourself."

"I can't help it. I've replayed it all a thousand times. Logically I know it wasn't my fault. But I can still hear the frantic pinging of their hearts on the monitor and know that I killed them."

I dry my eyes and look away.

Luanne sniffles and withdraws her arm from my shoulder. "Something happened to me, too. Something bad."

I hand her a tissue, then brush the hair from her forehead.

Pain pinches Luanne's face as she turns toward me. "I told you over a year ago that when I turned fifteen my parents held my Quinceañera, a big thing in Mexican culture where you become an adult. Friends, family, food, music, and drink. What more would you need for a great Mexican celebration? I guess everything except my boyfriend, Pablo. My dad always hated him and probably for a good reason. Pablo was always in trouble—one step away from jail. But, I was young, stupid, and totally in love. Daddy was old and judgmental. I mean, what could he know about love, right?"

With my arm across Luanne's shoulder, I feel her shiver even though it is warm inside. She takes a deep breath. "After the party was over, when my parents went to bed, I snuck out of the house to meet Pablo. He was waiting for me around the block in his car. From the beginning of our relationship, he had been after one thing, sex. But what guy isn't? Being a good girl, I planned on saving myself for marriage. Great plan but the wrong guy.

"He drove me out to a secluded grove at the lake. It was the usual routine that night, him trying to get in my pants and me trying to keep him out. Usually, it was a playful thing. But that night, he was drunk and angry, and it wasn't a game anymore. He ripped my shirt and slacks off. Held me down. And raped me."

My heart breaks as Luanne drops her hands helplessly in her lap. "But, the worst part was to come. I found out a month later that I was pregnant." A dark wave passes across Luanne's face. "I don't know if Daddy was more ashamed than furious, but he pressured me into an abortion. Save the family from humiliation. I should have stood up to him, kept the baby, but I was weak and agreed.

"After the abortion, I begged the nurse to tell me the sex of the infant. She said it was better not to know, but I insisted.

Finally, she told me it was a girl. My dead child was a girl. I should have fought Father, but I couldn't stand up to him, and I've carried the guilt ever since."

Luanne's shoulders heave, and soul-shaking sobs wrack her slender body. She brings her hands to her mouth and gasps. "That's what Stan forced me to remember, the memory of death and all the pain that goes with it."

Jacqui hugs Luanne tight. "I understand."

The living room is uncomfortably quiet until the air conditioner kicks in. A cool breeze emerges from the vent, ruffling our hair. The grandfather clock in the corner ticks the time away as we wait for Jacqui to begin.

"I had a twin sister named Christine, who was blind at birth. As early as I can remember, we had an awesome connection. You've probably heard of the psychic bond between twins? Well, we had it. If I was in pain, Christine felt it, then would tell me where it hurt, touching the same spot. She told me that she could take it away if I would concentrate on the sound of her voice."

Fierce intensity crosses Jacqui's face as she speaks, "My sister would start talking and place her hands on the area that hurt. The location would tingle, turn warm, and slowly cool until the soreness was gone. From an early age, she practiced psychic energy work before we even knew what the term meant."

Jacqui smiles at me, still deep in the memory. Then, she clenches her fists. "A few weeks after our fourteenth birthday, the whole family went camping in the rugged Sangre de Cristo mountains near Taos, New Mexico. We drove to the campsite in the National Park and set up the tent that afternoon. Because of some spoiled food, Mom and Dad had to make a trip back to town. They left me in charge of Christine, who was lounging in a camp chair and humming to herself.

"There was a nearby gorge, and I've always enjoyed the sound of rushing water. Assuming Christine was safe, I just had to explore on my own." Jacqui clenches her jaw. "I climbed down the thirty-foot stone face and crossed the rushing stream by stepping on the exposed rocks. But, something inside alarmed me, and I looked at the ledge above. Christine stood on the edge, oblivious to the danger below. She poised there and held out her hand. A brilliant hued butterfly landed on her palm. Then another and another, until they covered her from head to toe with colorful wings. Wings that gently opened and closed as Christine stood perfectly still.

"She had the uncanny ability to connect with nature, and this was a surreal meeting of humanity and the natural world until a breeze came upon her. A thousand butterflies took wing, swirled upward in a glorious riot upon the wind, colors flashing in the sun, leaving my sister bare of their presence. I looked at Christine and screamed for her to stop. She was following the butterflies, and the rushing water muffled my warning. A part of me perished that day when she plummeted to the stream below. My sister died when her head hit a rock.

"Since then, I've been tortured by the "what if" game. What if I'd watched Christine closer? What if she'd heard my scream and stopped? My thinking mind always conjures up a happy ending where Christine lived. But, for the rest of my life, I'll carry the guilt of not acting upon my what if."

My heart stutters as Jacqui lowers her head in shame. "I'm not the only one who was responsible for the death of someone they loved."

29

THE POWER OF THREE

AS WE SIT ON THE couch in the living room, Jacqui and Luanne's faces are tainted with despair. Their overpowering sadness generates a pain deep within my chest and threatens to engulf me. But I know I need to focus on them and will myself above the anguish, pushing back my emotions.

My hands shake as I look into their eyes. "So we each believe that we were responsible for the death of someone we loved."

The silence is oppressive as I stand before my two friends. "I feel guilty for killing my parents. For Luanne, it was your unborn child. And Jacqui, your twin sister, Christine."

Luanne hugs herself and rocks back and forth. Jacqui bangs her fist against the couch cushion.

I listen to the breaths of my two friends—short, swift, and fueled by fear. "What have these memories done to us? Why did Stan bring them to mind?"

Jacqui stops pounding the cushion. "We're a team, aren't we? The Triumvirate of Sisters?" She inhales deeply, releases it, furrows her brow. "What better way to break us down than to divide us through the memory of our guilt. Guilt over something we couldn't control."

Luanne clasps her hands and leans forward. "When your

team loses its focus, it can't come together. After that happens, you're no threat to the enemy."

My friends are on board now, and I lead them to a pivotal question. "Why would Stan go to so much trouble to divide us? Isn't Satan all powerful? Couldn't he think us dead or send his demons after us?

I snap my fingers and startle my friends. "No, there's a reason why he doesn't—or maybe he *can't.* So we need to start with the obvious—assess our powers. Powers that we may take for granted but could also be protecting us."

Luanne lifts her chin and catches my eye. "As you know, I'm able to alter a person's memory. Like change it—plant whatever I imagine in their mind."

Jacqui acknowledges with a whistle. "Why do you have all the flash, Luanne? Compared to yours, mine has always been downright boring."

Luanne stages a fake yawn. "I'll be the judge of that."

"Well, all I can do is talk to dead people. But I also have special insight into people's motivations from a special angel that watches over me."

I touch Jacqui's arm. "I never knew about your guardian angel. Would she be named Christine?" Jacqui's face twists in surprise and confirms my question.

"So, Archer,"—Jacqui taps her chin with her forefinger and deflects further discussion about Christine—"other than being a multi-gifted psychic, is there anything else you can do?"

"Since we last met in Costas's psychic enhancement class on Earth, I've added two extraordinary powers."

The girl's faces are bright and eager.

"I can… stop time."

Their eyes open wide.

"And I can kill with my mind."

Jacqui bolts upright. "Stop time. Kill a man. Really? I will never, *ever* piss you off, Archer."

"Well, technically, I haven't killed anyone yet, but I was just a heartbeat away from offing Allen Costas."

Luanne steeples her fingers and arches an eyebrow. "When did this happen?"

"Well, Costas had fled from the authorities after ordering Le Cadavre to substitute the poison that I administered to Mom and Dad. The director was hiding in a Florida beach house, and I psychically connected with him as he slept and nearly killed him with my mind."

I sit down next to Luanne. "So, yes, I can kill someone just by thinking it. And I pray to God I never have to."

Luanne clears her throat. "I just noticed something that might be important. Our powers fall into three categories."

Jacqui lifts one finger. "Communicating with the dead is in the spiritual realm."

Luanne smiles and holds up two fingers. "Controlling a mind is a mental activity."

I complete the list by extending three fingers. "Stopping time and psychically killing someone has a physical result."

A thought blossoms in my brain, and the breath catches in my throat. "Luanne, Jacqui, stand up and form a ring with me. Hold hands and be sure your palms touch. The Triumvirate of Sisters has three separate, distinct powers, and it's not by chance that the devil has attacked us."

The sound of street traffic filters through the walls, and the AC kicks in. The grandfather clock shows an hour has passed since we arrived.

"I want each of you to concentrate upon your psychic ability and see what happens when we combine our mental, physical, and spiritual powers."

We relax and focus inwardly. After a minute, three small explosions short out the fuse box, and the room goes dark. The girls' eyes widen in fear. The AC cuts off, the clock pendulum stops, and the air above us hums with an electrical charge. Then, a blinding glow blasts through the room, bathing us in white.

I can't believe what I see.

30

SEE ME, FEEL ME,
TOUCH ME

THE VERY FABRIC OF MY alternate parents' house quivers as the white light surges. The celestial beam penetrates the walls, silently disintegrating the paneling and sheetrock, then clears away the wooden studs.

The light dissolves the concrete foundation beneath our feet and drains the refuse downward into a swirling, vortex of spiritual energy. My two friends and I are safe, suspended in the eye of this storm, still holding hands, hair, and clothes whipped by the divine force we've summoned.

We are surrounded, supported by, and entombed within the brilliant fabric of a Godly cocoon, brought about by our combined thoughts. Luanne and Jacqui's eyes are still closed, and no sound breaches my ears as I decipher the Lord's Prayer upon their moving lips.

An internal feeling comes softly as cat's feet in the darkness and curls comfortably around the base of my mind. Power infuses my body as a nameless source speaks in the verbal coin of the angels, "Blessed are the searchers, for they shall find that which they seek." The spiritual power of these words resonates upon the warp and woof of my soul, in the deepest manner imaginable.

Surprisingly, I have no fear as the circular wall of white

fabric draws closer, moving toward the calm eye where it gently holds us.

A sacred presence resonates within my mind before giving voice. "The faithful fear not, for they shall repel the swords and daggers of evil and destroy the unholy force that challenges them." I have never felt so alive and energized. Boundless love embraces my soul, flushes my consciousness with astounding clarity.

I am in the presence of God's Holy Word and stand in awe. Yet, my question remains, how do we engage the power of the Three Sisters?

"Before you approach the Throne, purify yourself. Then all knowledge shall be yours." The heavenly voice pulses within my mind.

The walls of the silken fabric now embrace me, Jacqui, and Luanne. My two friends are unaware of their surroundings, yet their lips still move in private prayer. The gossamer essence touches us and shimmers on our skin. It is then my mind knocks upon the hidden door.

It opens upon a divine image, and I mentally step inside a vaulted chamber—a chamber unadorned yet alive and vibrant, exuding a presence of its own. Its hidden power whispers of buried memories from my past. Former victories, forgotten defeats, lies, and layered truths, all intertwined within the tapestry of my life.

Intuitively, I know that to approach God's Throne, I must center myself and summon my spiritual ideal—love—and then focus on the feeling that rises within. I imagine it, then sense its sacred force traveling through my gut, extending to my limbs, culminating at the top of my head.

My breathing is slow and deep, my concentration crystallized upon the rising power as it disseminates through my body.

The aura of divine presence seeps into my soul and layers my consciousness with the presence of God. I ride upon magnificent waves of spirituality, buoyed up with the company of truth and purpose.

My critical mind is far away, my focus sublime, and nothing stands in my way.

Nothing.

Until my world crashes down upon me.

31

DARKNESS AND DESPAIR

MOMENTS BEFORE, I WAS HOLDING hands with Jacqui and Luanne and forming a sacred circle to enlist Heavenly guidance to defeat Stan's plan to reign destruction over four more worlds. Our combined psychic powers created a spiritual synergy and nearly brought us answers.

But now, I'm all alone and falling through darkness so black, so hideous, that if sunlight breached its border, it would be sucked into oblivion, leaving no trace, no warmth, no hope. My shimmering bubble of spirituality has collapsed, and the Godly cocoon that once protected me, purges itself of my presence. The aura of love that led my quest for spiritual direction now withers upon the cruel wind rushing past my body.

My sense of time distorts. Seconds pass like hours, and I continue to fall until oily tendrils from the surrounding gloom grasp my body. They ease my momentum from terrifying freefall into a controlled descent. Finally, I'm motionless—suspended in this pit of despair.

Indistinct words, birthed by unseen lips, whisper at my ear. I strain to decipher their meaning, leaning forward to catch a phrase. Recognition eludes me, and I am left to absorb the presence of evil that permeates this ungodly place. My heart thunders violently, a ragged primal beat in response to raw fear—fear that fuels my harsh, savage breath.

Dark wraiths trail gossamer webs over my face and body. I try to raise my hands to wipe them away and shriek in horror. But, my cry dies a twisted death upon the fabric of unholiness that surrounds me. Terror explodes through my core and feeds the frenzy of the dark murmurs.

Piercing the disturbing whispers, a distant pounding repeats slowly, incessantly. Each forceful impact squeezes the breath from my lungs and causes the cauldron of darkness I'm suspended in to roll like a tide, pushing me toward the deadly concussion.

I'm drug down this vile passage, toward the source of the violent beat, pinned in place by supernatural, ebony bonds. Awful whispers, louder now, are enraged with malice and target me like a predator in the night.

"Kill the bitch!" Shrill voices strafe my ears with barbed intensity. "We never wanted you here."

The violent hammering is coming closer, deafening me as the black, waterless tide drags me closer to a violent death. Even though I cannot see the pounding mechanism, I imagine two opposing walls colliding against each other, mashing whatever falls between them. As I struggle against the restraints that hold me in place, my muscles cramp from the strain.

Why am I here? Is this Stan's malicious plan? A way to end the Triumvirate of Sisters? The darkness I'm entombed in and the malevolent voices around me are the projection of undeniable evil—an evil that wants me dead.

The irresistible force pushes me to the edge of the unseen death machine until I rest upon its lip. The energy is too strong to resist, but I fight for my life. Try to kick my feet, try to twist my body, try to avoid the inevitable. I'm seconds from falling. And I don't want to die. Not in this place. Not in this way. I want to live. I want to see my baby born.

Looking upward into the unforgiving darkness, I plead to a God who seems to have forgotten me, then curl forward to protect my unborn child. With one final scream, I'm drug into the abyss below.

32

LET THERE BE LIGHT

MY SCREAM SMOTHERS IN THE suffocating darkness as I plummet downward. Yet, the horrid tendrils that once bound me are now distant memories, and I can finally move my limbs. Twisting my body to protect my unborn baby from the coming impact, I tense for the inevitable.

A small halo of light cuts through the gloom, and my heart drums a bastard rhythm, the breath bumps up my throat. I reach upward and no longer feel the wind rushing past my body. There is a firm foundation against my back and legs, and I'm no longer falling. Thank God I'm still alive!

The light is brighter now, and I blink against the glare. Gradually, two faces come into focus. Two faces that belong to my two best friends. Jacqui and Luanne.

Luanne bends down and helps me sit up.

"What happened? Are you okay? You passed out on us."

I place my trembling hands upon the floor of my alternate parents' home and breathe deep. A quick look around, and everything is still in place, the walls, ceiling, and foundation are all intact. Just like it was before we joined hands and combined our powers.

"I'm fine now." The lie comes easily, but inside, I'm not fine. I'm scared. Putting my game face on, I look up at Jacqui, then Luanne. "What do you remember after we joined hands and closed our eyes?"

Jacqui crosses her arms. "Well, I concentrated on combining our mental, physical, and spiritual abilities, just like you said to."

Luanne nods her head. "So did I."

"And then what happened?" I search their faces for a glimmer of recognition—anything to explain what just occurred to me.

Jacqui frowns. "I focused inwardly for ten or fifteen seconds, and then you fell to the floor."

Luanne turns her inner arm toward me. "I have scratch marks from your nails when you went down."

Holy shit! I look at her red marks and don't remember a thing. But, more alarming is the fact that my friend's fifteen seconds extended into an eternity of horror and near death for me. Without sharing my experience of expanded time, I tell them about my spiritual journey—a quest for direction to defeat Stan, my fall through terrifying darkness, and escaping death in the crushing pit.

I pause a moment, running my hand through my hair. "Stan has to be behind my failure to attain Divine guidance. Because he's the only one who would benefit from it."

"That could be true." Luanne clenches her fist. "While we were focusing with our eyes closed, was he controlling your mind?"

"If Stan had been controlling me mentally, I could have resisted his power. So, he couldn't have hurt me physically. Frightened me, yes. But harm me, no." In a moment of reflection, I feel the pulse of hidden truth. "Somehow, he hijacked my astral body."

The question on Jacqui's face leads me to explain. "The astral body is somewhere between the soul and physical body and can travel at will to any location it desires."

Jacqui turns to face me. "If Stan was directing the black tide that pulled you toward the killing machine, what would have happened if your astral body died?"

"My real body back on Earth would die, too."

Horror savages my friends' faces—emphasizes how close to death I'd been. I stand up and dust off my slacks. "I'm grateful to be still alive. But why in the hell didn't Stan kill me when he had the chance?"

33

DOUBLE DOWN, DAWG

JASON BLAINE SLAMMED DOWN A three thousand dollar shot of Stan's 1937 Glenfiddich whiskey and glared at the blackjack dealer. Just like Blaine, the card handler was tall and muscular, had brown hair, and an overdose of Nazi insignia tattooed across his arms and shaved head.

Here, in the dark, remote Texas countryside, in a fortified retreat, far from the authorities, Jason and thirty freed felons were celebrating to the max. Tonight's menu included drugs. More drugs. Lots of sex. Overpowering music. And gambling.

But, ten minutes ago, a dark wave of impending violence stopped the drug use, sent the hookers running, and tainted the ragged rhythm of rock and roll.

But it didn't stop the gambling.

Even the most hardened criminal present was uneasy by Blaine's growing aura of rage.

At the edge of Stan's expansive gambling pit, music blared from a six-million-dollar Kipnis Outer Limits theatre system, adding to the sense of agitation until someone turned it off. The absence of sound pounded the room into submission as Blaine studied the dealer's exposed card.

A seven of hearts.

Blaine's losses were now over a hundred thousand, and the

card handler smirked. "Hey, Bro, the odds favor the house. If I were you, I'd cut bait."

This wasn't a good time to double down, but Blaine dropped another thirty thousand beside his original bet. "Fuck you and your advice."

The observers moved closer, marinating the stench of un-washed bodies with expensive liquor. Even the most drugged-out felon seemed to know Jason Blaine was fighting a raging cauldron of repressed savagery. Savagery ready to explode.

The onlookers realized the dealer was cheating. And from the guilty look on the card handler's face, Blaine knew it, too.

Upon their afternoon arrival at the remote complex, Stan had staked all thirty-one felons with two hundred thousand, along with the promise that when Earth and the alternate worlds were attacked, another million in gold would be their final payment.

For now, Blaine looked at two issues—losing his money and being cheated.

But he couldn't prove the latter. Not yet.

The dealer flipped Blaine's hole card over, turned a king of spades from the deck, and placed it next to the seven of diamonds.

Blaine's count stood at seventeen. And his gut told him it wasn't good enough.

The dealer showed his cards—seven of hearts and ace of clubs. "Bro, you should have listened. House's eighteen beats your seventeen." The card handler raked Blaine's sixty thousand to his side.

Twenty-nine pairs of eyes followed Blaine's hand as he jerk-ed a 9mm Glock from his waistband.

"I just figured it out. How you cheated me."

The dealer put both hands up, and his mouth opened in surprise. "Brother, I wouldn't cheat you. I was looking at life in Clements. Why would I fuck with the golden goose?"

Blaine moved the gun slightly, locking eyes with his target. "Unbutton your left sleeve and roll it up."

"Look, I'll give the money back." The dealer's eyes flitted from Blaine's gun to the pile of cash on his side. "Take my two hundred K. And your losses. Just don't pull the trigger."

Blaine went rock hard as he shoved the gun forward. "Shut your fucking mouth. And roll up your sleeve."

The dealer's hands shook as he unbuttoned his cuff and lifted the material. A rubber band held four cards in place against his inner arm.

"Spread 'em out."

The dealer's hands trembled as he laid them on the black-jack table.

Blaine narrowed his eyes. "Two kings and two aces make a winning hand every time."

"Look, Jason, I was just playing with you. I was gonna give it back. You know me, know how I like to joke. Right?"

"So, you'd give me my losses and your two hundred K?"

"In a heartbeat, Bro."

The silence in the gambling pit was deafening. The onlookers began to back up.

Sweat rolled down the dealer's brow.

Blaine's finger tightened against the trigger.

"Don't kill me. I'm your flesh and blood, man. Doesn't that mean anything?"

Blaine knew their mother would kick his ass because he was going to kill her favorite son. But he hadn't given a damn what she thought in over twenty years. "Blood might be thicker than water, 'Bro,' but I can't spend blood."

The bullet exploded his brother's head, and in the blaze of the muzzle blast, Blaine fed off his audience, and the audience fed off him. In Blaine's world, no one would leave hungry tonight. For savage justice had been served to the living as a reminder to all—you don't fuck with the man.

IN THE REMOTE SECTOR OF Stan's compound, the devil heard the gunshot and flicked the closed-circuit television off. Tonight's drama confirmed his belief that he'd assembled the perfect team. A team that exceeded his expectations for brutality and mayhem. And Stan would use their violence until he couldn't use them anymore.

When God had expelled the devil from Heaven, He had decreed that the fallen angel could not physically act upon mankind. That is, Stan could not pull the trigger on the gun. However, he could influence those willing to do his dirty work. And that was why he needed Jason Blaine and his thirty felons. Under Stan's guidance, they would unleash havoc upon the four remaining worlds, and then he would manipulate them into untimely death as they finished off the planetary hit list.

It was time to celebrate his good fortune. So, the devil grabbed the TV remote, cued up his favorite episode of the *Love Boat,* and opened a Dollar Store bag of expired Cheetos.

Life was so good on so many levels. He smiled and shoved a handful of orange, crunchy nuggets in his mouth. And, sometimes, you just had to stop and smell the roses.

34

NOTHING PERSONAL,
IT'S BUSINESS

STAN WIPED A TEAR AWAY, snuffled into a Kleenex, and sighed as his *Love Boat* rerun ended. Even though he ruled Hell with an iron fist, romantic comedies brought out his softer side. Sucking the orange Cheeto crumbs off his fingers, he glanced at his watch. Anticipating Jason Blaine any moment, the devil was aware of the felon's plan to overthrow him and take the reins of Hell.

The devil had been generous to Blaine by springing him from jail, reuniting him with old associates, as well as laying some serious money on him. What the felon failed to understand was that the devil had the power to see the treachery within.

Even though the river of darkness ran swift and deep within Blaine, Stan was the river, the singular source of all evil. The felon was heading toward a train wreck and didn't even know it.

The devil rose when someone knocked on his door, then rubbed his hands together in glee. Always one to set up contingency plans, the first scheme was to set Jason Blaine up so skillfully that the criminal wouldn't know what hit him. Ironically, the devil would not kill Blaine after he and the team attacked the remaining four worlds. No, with information gathered tonight, the State of Texas could apprehend the convict, strap him to the lethal injection table, and snuff out his worthless life. That was only one of several options on the table for the clueless felon. And only time would reveal the course of action.

"COME IN." THE DEVIL ROSE to meet his guest.

Blaine opened the door and sauntered across Stan's media room. Three rows of high-end recliners set in front of a massive movie screen that was scrolling the closing credits to the *Love Boat*.

"Did I interrupt something?" Blaine's eyes flickered with mirth, but he kept the grin off his face.

Stan coughed, adjusted his pocket protector, and shoved up his black, horned-rim glasses. "Just doing research." He turned away and powered the unit off.

"What's on your mind?"

Stan rose to his full height and still had to look up at Blaine. The devil could have chided himself for manifesting as a harmless accountant. But there was a mental mojo behind his madness. Rather than show himself as a seven-foot demon chewing on a severed limb, Stan preferred to lull his audience into a false sense of security.

Who was afraid of pencil pushers? Unless they worked for the IRS, bookkeepers didn't instill fear.

Cultivating a noncritical, dull demeanor was what Stan tried to achieve. Because when he removed the mask and became the godless ghoul, gnawing on a hunk of fresh meat, the contrast between a mild accountant and mega-monster would magnify horror into epic proportions.

After his team of escaped felons assaulted the four remaining worlds, Stan would reveal his true self to Jason Blaine. But first, the devil needed to solidify his control over his willing henchman.

Stan handed Blaine a .38 Special and pointed toward a

door next to the movie screen. "I want you to kill the man inside that room."

"Anyone I know?"

"The name Raptor ring a bell?"

Blaine cracked his knuckles. "Can I ask why?"

"Does it matter?"

The felon opened the .38's cylinder and checked the cartridges, then snapped the chamber shut and smiled a cold, predator's grin. "The Raptor and I have a history together. My organization supplied him with cocaine, and he gave me prison info."

Stan's lips curled downward. "And your point is?"

"Is this personal or business?"

"Make it whatever you want, son."

While Blaine ambled toward the door, Stan removed his iPhone and tapped the closed-circuit TV app. Tonight, two murders committed by the escaped felon, Jason Blaine, would be recorded. And Stan planned to invoke his wrath against the potential usurper after he decided which path his punishment would take.

Stan had standards to uphold.

When you fuck with the devil, there was hell to pay.

35

BERRY BIG BALLS

STAN STOOD IN FRONT OF his four-man team in the media room the next morning at ten a.m. The devil had always been a Pee-wee Herman fan and was pleased to welcome the actor's clone in this morning's crew.

Kra-zee Sherman, one of four felons selected to assault an alternate world in thirty minutes, got his nickname in prison decades ago from his bizarre interpretation of the real Pee-wee Herman. Thanks to Stan's massive collection of thrift store clothes, Kra-zee was dressed like the comedy star, sporting a snappy grey sports coat, high-waisted polyester pants, a white dress shirt, and the iconic red bowtie.

But his facial embellishments were what put the Kra-Kra in Kra-zee. The imitator had applied blood-red lipstick, then extended it from the corners of his lips up to his cheekbones. His bizarre grin was further enhanced with freshly shaved eyebrows that were replaced halfway up his forehead with black magic marker.

He lit up a Lucky Strike, took a deep drag, and blew smoke in the faces of the three team members.

Even though Kra-Kra was small and punched the scale at one twenty, the other men ignored the insult. Stan had read the imitator's rap sheet and was impressed. Kra-zee was the alpha male in the prison dog pound because he was crazy fast with a knife. Twenty years ago, the unintimidating felon had slashed four aggressive bikers in a bar fight that started when he ordered a glass of warm milk. The confrontation lasted less than one minute and left four Hell's Angels dead.

In tune with the crew's thoughts, Stan understood that in their world, violence ruled. And Kra-zee Sherman was the undisputed king. So, if he wanted to blow smoke in his follower's faces, or even up their asses, they willingly closed their eyes, held their breath, and clenched their teeth until it was over.

Kra-Kra turned to the three team members and snapped his fingers. Their heads twisted around. "Whenever you hear the magic word, 'balls,' clap like you mean it."

Stan cleared his throat, waited for a beat, then acknowledged the men with a nod. "This morning I'm sending you on a mission to purge the first location on an alternate world."

One felon spread his hands as his brow furrowed. "We got a small team if we're gonna use guns and explosives."

Stan gestured toward a compact box on the media room's walnut table. "You'll use this destabilizing igniter, which will make the air molecules flammable and cause the atmosphere to explode in a five-mile radius. Within sixty minutes all living things will be incinerated, leaving a smoldering dead mass."

"How do we get to the first hit, Stan?" Kra-zee crossed his arms and grinned.

"There are two methods. We can create a physical portal between our world and the target planet. This method takes time, which we don't have. Because any disruption of alternate worlds is monitored by Tara the Traveler, whose job is to protect the integrity of the multiverse. Even though I'm a fallen angel, I can still access the Hallway of Infinity. Once there I'll open the door to the alternate planet, you men will plant the device, set the switch, and leave immediately."

One congested team member clenched his fist and shook it. "You got berry big balls, Stan."

The team erupted in wild applause over the use of the magic word, and Kra-Kra jumped up and down.

Stan took a bow. "Well, then, gentlemen, let's get our asses in gear."

36

THIRTY WHAT?

"BRING THE DESTABILIZING IGNITOR." STAN gestured toward the small, coffin-like device resting on the table.

Kra-zee Sherman and the other three men grabbed the handles on either side of the box and lifted. "Got it. Now, how do we get to the bitchin' target?"

"This way."

The four-member destruction crew followed Stan as he walked past three rows of high-end recliners to the media room's back wall. The devil stopped, placed a forefinger against each temple, and concentrated. For the next minute, the rhythmic breathing of five men whispered against the silence, until one crew member gasped.

He pointed at a doorknob that had materialized in the middle of the bare wall. Astonishment spread across the team's faces as a line began at the base of the sheetrock, extending in a rectangular shape by going up, across, and down the wall until a door appeared.

Kra-zee leaned closer and touched the wood with his free hand. "Holy shit! How the hell did that happen?"

Stan took a deep breath. "One of the few perks of being a fallen angel is that I'm allowed access to an infinite number of worlds."

"Is that what's in there? Other worlds?"

"Let's take a look." Stan opened the door and motioned the team inside.

The men walked across the threshold and looked both ways. Overhead lights extended into infinity, in both directions, illuminating beige doors spaced seven feet apart.

Kra-zee's upper lip trembled. "What the fuck is this?"

"The Hallway of Infinity." Stan waved his hand to the left, then the right.

"What's behind the doors?"

"Behind an infinite number of doors lies an infinite number of worlds." Stan reached for one of the beige doorknobs. "And we don't have much time. If Tara the Traveler shows up, the party's over. So, let's get started with the demolition."

Stan opened the door, and saltwater spray washed over them. One hundred yards ahead, waves crashed against a rocky shoreline, sending mist into the air. Overhead, gulls cried out as they rode the wind coming off the sea. Just one mile away across the bay was a thriving metropolis.

"We don't have much time. So, take the destabilizing ignitor to the edge of the rocks, just before the ledge drops to the water." Stan pointed, and the men's eyes tracked to the spot.

Kra-zee wiped the salt spray from his brow. "Once we get there, how do we set the machine?"

"You'll press this knob." Stan motioned to a round, black button in the middle of the device.

"How long do we have before it ignites the air?"

"A digital readout above the button will start at thirty minutes and begin counting down toward destruction. More than enough time to get back to me."

The team looked at Kra-zee for confirmation, then hustled across the rocky terrain.

Within a few minutes, they reached the edge of the cliff, then pressed the ignition knob.

The four men stared at the countdown display, looked back at Stan, then began running toward the door. Their piercing primal screams sent a shiver of satisfaction through Stan's heart.

Twenty yards away, Kra-zee shrieked, "You set that mother fucking timer for thirty seconds. I'm going to cut your balls off, you bastard!"

Stan closed the door on his doomed team and was the only one who acknowledged the magic word. The only one who appreciated the irony. The only one who was left to clap.

A bone-crushing, ballbusting explosion battered the closed door, and Stan put his hands together, applauding in tribute to Kra-zee Sherman.

The sound echoed down the Hallway of Infinity as Stan stepped back into his media room. Not only had he saved four million dollars by indirectly killing the team, but he'd just bombed the hell out of one unsuspecting city.

Five down. Three to go.

37

KNOCK, KNOCK.
WHO'S THERE?

I'M SITTING ON THE COUCH with Jacqui and Luanne when someone knocks on my alternate parents' door.

"I've got it, girls." I step across the living room rug, past the grandfather clock, into the entryway to open the screen. Tenkiller, the blind, six-foot eight-inch monolith stands humbly with hands together, holding the leash to his four-pound service dog, Rambo. The NFL linebacker lookalike has changed his wardrobe from Army surplus overcoat to a woman's fuchsia sweatshirt with hot pink polyester pants. Unfortunately, the slacks stretch to bursting, and the cuffs come to mid-calf.

I guide him over to my friends.

The fallen angel extends his hand.

Both Jacqui and Luanne greet him, then scoot over to make room on the couch.

I reach across and touch his massive forearm. "What brings you here?"

"You've told Jacqui and Luanne about my involvement?"

"Yes, and they're on board to stop Stan."

Tenkiller's shoulders slump. "Since we last talked, Stan slipped into the Hallway of Infinity this morning and made another hit. The team that set the demolition device died in the explosion."

"That's five worlds the devil's assaulted." I look up into his sightless eyes. "How do we stop him, Ten?"

"He has to go back to the Hallway to access three more worlds. So, I suggest that you and your friends hitch a ride with me and wait in the Timekeeper's apartment. Once we get there, I'll tell you my plan on how to stop him, quickly and permanently."

"I'm ready if you are." I rise, and Jacqui and Luanne follow. We look at Tenkiller for direction.

He senses our attention and nods his head. "Jacqui, watch Rambo, and the rest of you move close together. Hold hands and repeat after me, O Father, who art in Heaven, deliver us to the hallowed ground where we may vanquish Satan. And may you guide us along thy way with a fuller sense of truth, justice, and the promise of a better day."

In the blink of an eye, we're all standing in the Timekeeper's apartment, and I gasp as I look around. The living room is a mess. Furniture has been turned over, worktable drawers ripped out, and papers scattered across the floor.

It has to be the work of Stan because the obscenity painted on the wall hardens my heart and rips it out completely. Slashing strokes of red drag my soul to the depths of despair.

In a few days, there'll be room in Hell for all of us.
Love, Mom, and Dad.

I don't care if he *is* the devil. And it doesn't bother me that he has the upper hand. But what does concern me is holding him responsible for needless destruction and the massacre of innocent life.

My eyes tear over, and my stomach churns. It's then I vow upon all that is holy to rip out Stan's putrid organs, grind them into a fine paste, and set fire to the remains—all while keeping him alive as long as possible.

"It's not going to be that easy, Archer." Tenkiller covers my hand with his. "But, I do have a plan that will work."

Not only is Ten good at reading minds, but his timing is impeccable. I intertwine my fingers with his and hold tight. Looking up into his sightless eyes, I wonder what blinded this gentle spirit. How did he end up with a four-pound, ill-tempered service dog, and why the hell is he dressed in hooker's clothes?

38

A SMALL BLADDER

TENKILLER STANDS TO MY LEFT in the Timekeeper's apartment, with arms crossed and boots firmly planted upon the living room carpet. Jacqui and Luanne are nearby and lean forward.

I'm curious about Ten's statement. Specifically, how to keep Stan from attacking the last three worlds. The sooner he shares that with us, the better for everyone involved.

"So, Ten, what's your plan?"

"It's simple and quick. And will bring the devil down, hard."

The fallen angel takes a deep breath and stands straighter, causing his head to brush against the popcorn ceiling. He flicks a fallen flake from his shoulder and wrinkles his brow. "I'm surprised I didn't think of it sooner."

I steeple my fingers and nod. "Don't keep me waiting, let's hear the details."

"Well, the most important element involves you and—"

Rambo jerks against his leash and gives a guttural growl followed by a high-pitched yip.

Ten stops and shakes his head. "Sorry, but that's Rambo's cue to go pee. Any suggestions where I can find a yard full of grass?"

"Something like a nice park?"

"Yep. And it's gotta be quick." The angel dips his head in

embarrassment. "I've never accessed an alternate world, so how do I navigate the system?"

"Go back out the living room door and turn left into the Hallway of Infinity. Then concentrate on what you want like a big patch of fescue. If you can imagine it, you can access it. So, follow your intuition to the correct door, and your desire will manifest itself in an alternate world."

Tenkiller obediently follows his service dog to the Timekeeper's door, then out into the hallway.

He moves his head back inside and grins. "I'll be back soon, and then I'll tell you how to stop Stan."

A trickle of relief layers my thoughts with gratitude. We're getting close to derailing the devil, and nothing stands in our way.

Except for Rambo, apparently.

39

BEHIND THE MIRROR DARKLY

DURING THE LAST THIRTY MINUTES, Jacqui and Luanne have straightened up the Timekeeper's apartment and scrubbed Stan's red-lettered obscenity off the wall. For the fourth time in less than five minutes, I glance at my watch then decide to look for Tenkiller.

"Girls, wait here, I'll be back shortly."

As I step out of the Timekeeper's apartment, I look left then right and note an infinite number of doors. Doors that offer an infinite number of worlds. And an infinite number of possibilities where Ten and Rambo could be.

Looking at this logically, it makes sense that the angel and dog couldn't have gone far, so I step down the hallway and scan for a door that's ajar.

After twenty yards of inspection, I reverse direction and check the opposite side for an open entryway. Four doors down, I catch a lucky break. Pressing against the beige wood, I step inside and observe three incongruous elements. First, within Tenkiller's alternate world, lies an endless layer of lush grass. Secondly, the rich fescue surrounds a lone liquor store. And thirdly, two identical voices rise within the shop.

This world of Tenkiller's is more than a place for Rambo to pee. It has the feel of something deeper, more meaningful.

The fallen angel's commanding baritone rumbles with feeling as I hurry across the lawn and into the liquor store.

"Schwear, did I go wrong?"

Ten is drunk, and the pain in his voice ignites my emotion, then detonates my empathy and strafes my soul with his suffering.

I stand an arm's length from two massive ebony angels.

On my left. Tenkiller. In a fuchsia sweatshirt. And hot pink stretch-pants.

To my right. Tenkiller's doppelganger. In custom leather loafers. And a Saville Row suit.

Tenkiller lifts a fifth of gin to his lips and takes a hefty pull. "Jus wear did I go wrong?"

From the tone of his voice and the nearly empty bottle, my pinkalicious angel hasn't wasted any time in releasing his inner demon.

His opposite, Saville Row Savvy, sucks the orifice of a bottle of expensive French champagne. Single-mindedly, he sets sail through the bubbly sea of Dom Perignon before he berths the bottle and belches boldly.

"Where did you go wrong?" Ten's doppelganger pinches the bridge of his nose. "Like you just told me, that night, in your world, you checked on the family one last time before meeting with Colonel Landers. And before you left, Jacob, his parents, and siblings were safe."

"Thash right. They were okay. They were fine. All of them. Until they weren't."

"Then, the gas leak ignited and killed all of them."

Tenkiller slugs down the last swallow of gin, then drops the empty fifth upon the floor and cries. "I wasn't there for them. I let them die. I killed them."

Ten rubs tears away with his massive hand. "What happened to you, in your world? Did Jacob and hish family die too?" The drunken angel weaves, on the verge of passing out.

Handling his alcohol better, Ten's counterpart shrugs. "In my world, the kitchen stove's valve never malfunctioned, and there was no explosion. Jacob and his family lived. Today, the young man is one of God's prophets heralding His love through healing by the laying on of hands."

The doppelganger strokes his chin. "On second thought, it's peculiar that your Colonel Landers summoned you for a conference, drew you away from the house at a critical time. His action could be hiding an ulterior motive. Do you trust him, Ten?"

Ten reaches out to his doppelganger to steady himself. "Yesh, I trust him. Totally."

Saville Row Savvy puts his arm around Tenkiller. "Then this could be nothing more than an accident. You couldn't have stopped it. In your world, the family was meant to die."

"You say the family was meant to die? What kind of God schends innocent childrens to their death?"

"God's will works in mysterious ways." Saville Row Savvy grips Ten's forearm.

Like a massive tree felled by the logger's ax, the fallen angel hit the floor. Before passing out, he swears a string of curses against his fate

And the message of his profanity illuminates a belief that no one understands. No one listens. And no one gives a damn.

I fist my hand, gouging fingernails into soft flesh. Just moments ago, I was about to hear a foolproof plan to defeat the devil. And now, the source of the plan, a drunken angel, is sleeping off a gin, fifth full fiasco.

And I don't have a clue when he will come to.

40

YOU'VE GOT MAIL

LEE KALE HAD A PLAN to bring down Jason Blaine, and it was a damned good one. As the High-Security mailman, he was going to access the letters of Blaine's known associates and look for contact between the incarcerated offenders and the escapee, Blaine.

What he was about to do was illegal, and an abuse of power, but Lee had little choice. If he didn't stop Blaine, then his infant son would be slaughtered like the deer on his porch late last week. And if he decided to spill his guts to the prison officials, then he'd face criminal charges for helping the felon escape.

The death of his son would be unimaginable, and confessing to the authorities was a ticket to the prison playpen where he would be on the receiving end of sadistic affection. Lee had no desire to be the meat of the month and would take the path of least resistance and greatest benefit. And since he was the mail screener for High Security, he had access to all the offenders' incoming and outgoing correspondence. Adding another layer of protection, Lee's desk was one of six and situated in the rear corner of the small screening room away from curious eyes or unwanted attention.

Lee accessed the prison's restricted gang file for Blaine by typing in his incarceration number on the antiquated state computer. The machine digested the request, then divulged the names of known associates as well as the offender's personal history.

Lee glanced to his right at Beverly, the mail screener for the Psych Building. She smiled, and he returned the gesture before looking back at the names on Blaine's list.

All three offenders were in Alpha pod, Blaine's former location, and were as dangerous as they came. The first, Batson the Butcher, styled himself as a Nazi death camp guard. Showing no mercy to his victims, making no exceptions for young or old, male or female. He was passionate in his trade, following Blaine's orders with cold efficiency, never leaving incriminating evidence. That was until the authorities found his collection of victims' ears.

Lee shivered when he read that the DNA from the severed flesh matched fifteen buried corpses. The liberal Texas jury spared him from execution but handed down a sentence of three consecutive life terms plus fifty years. Batson the Butcher had been legally fileted, then weighed upon the scale of justice and would never see the free world again.

A second name appeared under Blaine's associates. The notorious eyeball collector, Mark Cothran. Lee had met Cothran two years ago when the offender received a package in High Security. A correctional officer had escorted Lee to Cothran's cell and opened the food slot in the middle of the door to receive the books. The serial murderer was small and well mannered, certainly not intimidating. But it was his comment to Lee that raped his sense of personal safety into submission.

The five-foot-four-inch felon stroked his chin, stepped close to where Lee could see him. Then, soft as a lover, whispered, "You have such… lovely eyes."

The emotion behind the words was sensual, provocative, meant to titillate. But the look on Cothran's face was the marriage of darkness and evil. Wantonness and cruelty. A black hole of depravity colored his countenance.

When Blaine wanted to make a personal statement among the criminal world, he set Cothran upon them so that everyone concerned would "see" his point.

After the authorities brought Cothran down, Lee had heard the corrections officers say that the killer had ten pairs of eyeballs sitting on his dresser. Cut from ten innocent victims whose greatest offense was having beautiful eyes.

Inside the mail screening room, the overhead AC kicked in and blew a lukewarm wave of air over Lee. He wiped the sweat from his brow and focused on the last of Blaine's associates.

Morgan Fairview III was an anomaly in the Texas penal system. Educated and well connected, his family had money. Lots of it. So much they were referred to as the J. Paul Gettys of Texas.

Upon graduation from prep school in 1985, Fairview the III earned a full ride scholarship to Texas A & M University in College Station, Texas. He graduated with honors in three years with a major in Finance and a minor in Accounting.

At the time of his graduation, a recruiter for the Federal Deposit Insurance Corporation knew he'd hit the jackpot when Fairview applied for an Assistant Bank Examiner position. The young man had presented a professionally accepted research paper at a management seminar at Kansas State University. The freshman from A & M spoke eloquently and succinctly to a room of Doctorates and graduate students and received a standing ovation at the end.

Lee looked up from the computer and quickly scanned the room. No one had noticed him, so he continued reading.

Because of Fairview's intelligence and commanding presence, the FDIC snapped him up and started him in the Houston, Texas, field office. In 1988, the country was in the middle of the Savings and Loan crisis, and the young financial examiner cut his teeth on the rotting carcass of failing S & Ls. As a release from the relentless pressure the FDIC applied on new assistant examiners, he acquired a taste for strippers and cocaine.

The young dynamo was on the banking fast track, looking at full financial examiner status with the FDIC a year earlier than normal. He had already received offers for vice-presidencies from numerous banks yet turned them down.

Perhaps it was the cocaine or just bad luck, but the day Fairview the III met Jason Blaine, his entire life went to hell. The young regulator, who had yet to come into the family fortune, had a thousand dollar a day cocaine habit and was offered unlimited coke if he would help Blaine launder his illegal drug money.

Fairview did his job well for years until the authorities turned one of Blaine's associates who ratted on the money laundering scheme.

Even with the full resources of his family, the young man still entered middle age while sitting in prison. But when Lee Kale looked at the release date for Fairview the III, he bit his tongue in surprise.

The computer narrative intimated that Blaine's money man still had the bank account numbers to his bosses' hidden millions. But the important point was, Fairview would be released tomorrow.

And Lee would be in place to follow Blaine's men when they picked the moneyman up at the Amarillo prison.

Not one to take vows lightly, Lee swore that when this was over. Blaine would either be dead or back in prison. And if he had his way, Lee would be the one to put a bullet in the felon's head, not once but twice.

Because evil like that was hard to kill.

41

LIGHTS OUT, NIGHT, NIGHT

JACQUI, LUANNE, AND I STAND in the Timekeeper's apartment facing the couch bed where we tucked in an unconscious Tenkiller. After he passed out in the liquor store, the three of us, along with Ten's doppelganger, brought him back to sleep off his bout of binge drinking.

"It's strange looking at your mirror image." The corners of Saville Row Savvy's lips turn down, and a tear comes to his eye. He straightens to his full height and takes a deep breath. "What's even stranger is the depth and breadth of our differences."

I glance over at the sleeping giant. "Listening to your conversation earlier, I realized Tenkiller's addictions were fueled by deep regret. He took personal responsibility for the deaths of ten family members. Because he was unable to cope with the guilt, he began a destructive, downward spiral involving drugs, sex, and alcohol."

"And then there was the timing of his meeting with Colonel Landers." Saville Row Savvy wipes his tears away.

"I know it looks suspicious that the family died after Ten left to meet with Landers, but as you said, accidents happen. Tenkiller had no control over the kitchen stove's faulty gas valve but still blames himself for not staying."

Saville Row Savvy shakes his head. "What a horrible

place to live. Where your brain can't deal with the grief and mind-numbing pain."

I look at Tenkiller again. "Even in his suffering, there is nobility."

Ten's doppelganger runs his hand across his jaw. "When I first met him an hour ago, I wondered why. Why did he summon me?"

"Because you are everything he's not. In your world, Jacob and his family survived. And you bask in the love of the Lord." I spread my arms. "My intuition says Tenkiller was drawn to that. It also tells me he desperately needed the affirmation of normality and spiritual stability in your life.

"As a psychic empath, I know that after he absorbed all the goodness you had to offer, he compared his life to yours. And that vicarious feeling of being you, being pure and favored by God, crashed around him when he remembered his drug, sex, and alcohol abuse."

I take a shaky breath, feeling the drum, drum, drum of my pulse. "That memory led Tenkiller to the comfort of a fifth of gin. This kind and suffering angel took responsibility for the deaths of the family. To me, his pain over the extinction of ten precious lives screams, 'I care.'"

The angel called Saville Row Savvy crosses his arms. "It's what a good angel does."

"What's that? Caring?"

"Yes, we were made by the Creator to look after our human charges. Most angels do it well. A few do it better than others. But Tenkiller has gone beyond that by holding himself accountable for ten untimely deaths. Unless his attitude changes, his self-imposed suffering will lead to his demise. In the heavenly world, the passing of an angel is extremely rare. In all of time it has only happened twice. God loves and protects his winged workers, but if one chooses death, there is no coming back. That spirit fades into oblivion. It no longer exists if that is its choice."

Saville Row Savvy turns to leave, and I face the passed-out Tenkiller. Watching his chest rise and fall, I take an afghan off the back of the couch and spread it over his massive torso. The rambunctious Rambo jumps upon his master's breast and growls in Ten's face Then plops down for a quick siesta.

Ten is the one with the plan to defeat Stan, so all I can do is watch and wait for him to come to. At the rate Stan is assaulting worlds, it had better be damn quick.

42

GOLD FEVER

STAN OPENED A DOOR AND motioned his crew of felons to cross the Hallway of Infinity. "Quiet, now." He put his forefinger to his lips so the three teams of four men each got his point. The devil closed the door behind the last one through, stepped across the hallway, and opened an entryway to the sixth world slated for chaos and mayhem.

The three teams each carried a small, two-hundred-pound W 64 nuclear warhead with an explosive yield of 600 tons of TNT. The weapon had been in production from 1972 until 1979 and totaled 153 units. Fortunately for Stan, his inside man at the storage facility had fabricated a clerical error, which allowed the devil to take possession of three nukes.

To make sure that happened, a lot of money changed hands. No questions were asked. And only Stan knew where the dissenter's bodies were buried.

The twelve men followed the devil through the door into a semi-circular anteroom with three entrances.

Stan swept his hand in an arc. "Behind each door is a location where you will deliver the warhead, set the timer, and return to me within thirty minutes. The nuclear devices will be detonated on top of three weakened tectonic plates, causing a chain reaction of earthquakes to destroy nearby dwellings and inhabitants."

One of the felons rubbed his fingers together. "When do we get paid?"

"You've already gotten a two hundred thousand dollar advance. And you want more?"

"But you promised each of us a million in gold."

The other men laughed at the indignant attitude.

Stan patted the man's shoulder. "Of course, I did. You look like a strong man to me. Strong enough to carry forty-eight pounds of gold bullion. At today's rate, that's a million dollars. And I'm adding another hundred thousand dollars as a gesture of goodwill."

The team broke out in cheers but quieted when Stan raised his hands.

"You can thank me later. Right now, it's time to deliver the bombs to each site, set the timers, and regroup back here."

Twelve felons, in three teams of four men each, surged toward their designated door, ready to blow the hell out of an undesirable, unsuspecting, and unprepared world.

Stan was one world closer to assaulting the remaining planets, the Triumvirate of Sisters was a joke, and no one stood in his way. All in all, his run of luck was unfucking believable.

TWO FINGERS OF
HOLY WATER

MIKE CARBONA, ONE OF JASON Blaine's freed felons and the leader of Stan's first team, opened the door to the alternate world's newest target. He and three other men held the ends of two wide nylon straps running beneath a five-foot nuclear device—a two-hundred-pound warhead capable of impacting the underlying tectonic plate and causing devastating earthquakes.

In conjunction with two more mini-nukes, that was exactly what Stan's three teams would do.

The men passed through the door and stepped onto the targeted planet's barren earth. Just fifty feet ahead was the beginning of a deep, natural rift, and Carbona took the lead. Stan had instructed him on where to place the first nuclear weapon.

Baked by the afternoon sun, the team reached the edge of the drop-off and set the bomb down.

Carbona shrugged off his backpack and dropped a metal stake. He pointed at the individual to his left. "Take the hammer inside my knapsack and drive this bitchin rod three feet into the ground."

"Right." The man removed the seven-pound hand sledge and slammed it against the head of the metal rod. In between blows, he exhaled harshly. "What's the game plan, Boss?"

"We're gonna set the timer, tie this rope to the doomsday

machine, and lower it to the bottom of the gorge. Then we get the hell out of here."

The felon put the finishing blows on the steel rod and wiped sweat from his brow. "Can we trust Stan?"

Carbona put his hands upon his hips. "I hear a four-man team left his compound earlier today. Kra-zee Sherman and his crew."

"Yeah." The sweating man dropped his hammer on the dirt. "Stan got with us about 11:00 this morning, but I never saw Sherman."

The leader snapped his fingers at a Hispanic male holding a large coil of rope. "Garcia, string that line through the stake's eye."

"Sure thing, *Jefe.*"

Carbona looked up at the sky and wiped the sweat from his eyes. "You know, I asked Stan where Kra-zee's team was. Said he'd paid them off, then supplied a ride to Mexico."

"Seems convenient. Do you believe him?"

"As far as I can. And that ain't sayin' much."

Garcia finished tying off the rope to the metal pin's round eye. Looked up at Carbona for direction. "What now, *Jefe?*"

"Take the free end of the rope, run it through the nylon strip's four hand grips so that it'll hold the bomb like a cradle."

The Hispanic dug through the pile of rope, grabbed the loose end, and threaded it through the grips. "Is the steel pin some kinda anchor?"

"Yeah, it keeps the bomb from hitting the stones below if we lose our grip." Carbona bent over and set the timer on the atomic bomb, then gestured for the three team members to grab the rope. With caution scourged by fear, they gently lowered the mini-nuke.

Minutes later, the bomb rested at the bottom of the gorge, setting upon the weakest point of the first underlying tectonic plate below.

A breathless Carbona slapped his men's shoulders and hurried them back to the dimensional door, back to safety, and hopefully back to a cool million in gold. However, expecting the worst from Stan, Carbona chambered a round in his semi-automatic and hid the weapon in his waistband.

When it came to money, Carbona's motto was, "In God We Trust." And if the rest don't pay, he'd play them an old song. Performed in the key of 9mm, the 3/4 time tune would be punctuated with staccato bursts of 7.5 grams of lead to the head. And if Stan wasn't dead after the first few bars, Carbona would deliver an encore.

However, if the fucking devil was immortal, two fingers of Holy Water along with a wooden stake might be a smart move.

44

THE LU, LU, LUV BOAT

THE DEVIL'S NEXT TEAM, HEADLINED by Stutterin' Sam, stood in front of the second door leading into the sixth planet slated for mayhem. This group of four felons, like the first crew, cradled a two-hundred-pound mini-nuke upon two nylon straps, with hand grips on each end.

The men stepped through the entryway onto the top deck of an expansive, gracefully appointed, luxury cruise ship.

"Well, if it ain't the lu, lu, luv boat." Sam led the team down the port side walkway toward the stern. When the four men passed a group of party-goers, dressed in tuxedoes and gowns, the alarmed people quickly turned away or cowered in fear.

The afternoon sun shone upon the passengers and the pur-veyors of doom. To Sam, this gig was just another job, but so far, it was the easiest money he'd ever signed on for.

He adjusted his hand grip and double-stepped to keep in pace with the other three men. Sam looked back at the person behind him. "When we finish, wa, wa, what you gonna spend your money on?"

"I'm takin' a plane to Mexico, where the sun's warm, and the liquor flows like water."

Tyree, the felon to Sam's right, spit over the handrail into the sea. "Me, I'm gonna do Vegas. Buy a two hundred square foot tiny house and play penny slots at the casinos."

The four-man demolition crew stopped at the back of the boat. Without looking, Sam reached up and set the timer on top of the bomb. Having been seen by dozens of passengers, he hoped for a few more minutes before armed security showed up.

"Move over to the handrail." Sam shuffled closer and looked at the timer. He'd left his glasses back at Stan's compound and couldn't tell if the display said five minutes or thirty.

Tyree rolled his eyes. "What's next?"

"On my count, pitch this bad boy overboard. One, two, *three.*" Sam lifted his side of the nuke.

Together, the four men heaved the weapon overboard and watched it bob in the water, slowly sink downward, then disappear in the brilliant blue sea.

Sam turned around and led his crew in a quick run back to the dimensional door. "In about ten minutes, the device will hit the seabed, and twenty minutes later, if I set the timer right, it'll explode."

Tyree's face lit up. "You never did tell me what you gonna do with your share of a million dollars."

Sam pounded down the walkway, the breath jolting from his lungs. "I'm going to marry one of the ugliest women I can find."

"Sam, you bein' crazy. Why you do that? Cause you gettin' enough money from Stan for a top shelf woman."

"Beautiful women see me as somethin' to use or somethin' to avoid. But paying attention to an ugly woman is like feedin' a stray dog. With patience and time, you gain her trust and get loyalty and affection. When it comes to me, an ugly woman recognizes a kindred spirit. Because we're both stra, stra, stray dogs."

The four men came to a halt in front of the dimensional door they'd just come through.

Sam looked ahead.

Things were about to go to hell.

And quickly.

Twenty feet down the walkway, a three-man security team approached with guns drawn. One of the personnel aimed at Sam. "Don't move, or I'll shoot!"

Stutterin' Sam stepped in front of his men, shielding them with his body. "Get inside the door, NOW!"

Three crew members scrambled through just as the armed man fired. Sam clutched his side. "Son of a bitch, I'm hit!"

Tyree grabbed Sam's shirt.

Yanked him through the door.

Slammed it shut.

GRUMMAN, THE CRUISE SHIP'S SECURITY chief, approached the closed utility door where four perpetrators had just entered.

One of his men reached for the knob. "Cover me."

Their weapons raised chest high, and forefingers tightened upon triggers. Breathing accelerated, and nervous sweat formed. The point man swung the door open.

Three trained professionals sucked in air. Cursed in unison. They stared at two mops standing in oversized buckets, a row of hand tools hooked upon a peg board, and two dozen rolls of toilet paper set on a wooden shelf.

The four men they pursued.

Vanished.

Gone without a trace.

Security guard Lars Nilsson, pushed against the panels, hoping to find a hidden exit. Instead, he encountered three very solid walls.

Nilsson punched the wood. "Grumann, what the fuck is going on?"

The blond haired, six-foot Nordic chief holstered his weapon. "If I knew, I'd tell you." The security commander surveyed the closet and shook his head in disgust. What should have been a textbook takedown was turning into a major clusterfuck. He put his hand to his forehead and tried to concentrate. But a distant rumble below the boat sent a disturbing vibration up his feet. And that vibration birthed a dark premonition.

Something bad was about to happen.

A lot of people were going to die.

And Grumann could be one of them.

Three-hundred yards away, a stadium-sized plume of water exploded upward, mushrooming into the air, blocking out the sun. In the twilight darkness, the rear end of the cruise ship pitched upward, thrown by a huge tidal wave generated beneath the sea.

Grumann fell forward, headfirst into the utility closet, followed by the door slamming behind him. In total darkness, he extended his hands to break the inevitable impact with the mops and closet walls.

Right after the underwater explosion, an unseen force raised the hair on his arms and pulsed across his body. The closet light flared brilliantly, then exploded. In that moment of brief illumination, the mops, buckets, and other contents faded away. The walls vanished in the light before darkness returned.

The crazy tilt of the cruise ship sent him farther into the darkened interior, much farther than what was possible. His mind reeled from the insanity of his situation. What should have been a three-foot by four-foot closet, was now an enormous cavern.

A huge, hideous hole.

The floor suddenly stabilized, and he nearly stumbled, caught himself, and stood erect. In the darkness ahead of him, he heard the shuffle of feet and the low murmur of men talking. His heart power-humped the inside of his chest when they opened a door.

Moving back into the shadows, he watched the perpetrators he'd tried to subdue help their bleeding comrade through the entryway into a small white anteroom.

Grumann didn't know where the hell he was, yet he thought about the passenger's reports of four men carrying a bomb down the port side walkway. The pulse he felt moments ago could have been a short burst of electromagnetic energy, which could have come from a low yield mini-nuke. That could explain his hair standing on end and the pulsing sensation across his body. But how did it erase the closet walls and equipment?

Something else was at work here, and Grumann knew to give it a rest. He reluctantly thought about the safety of his men, the crew, and five thousand passengers.

The Nordic security commander pulled his semiautomatic, flipped the safety off, and under cover of darkness, crept to the edge of the new exit. The four men, unaware of his presence, closed the door behind them.

Grumann gripped the inside knob and leaned close to the steel entrance. As he listened, beads of sweat rolled down his face, dropping to the floor. The voices on the other side continued to talk.

He moved closer.

One unseen man screamed, "Sam, you set the fucking timer for five minutes!"

"I took a bullet for you so that you could escape. And you're bi, bi, bitchin' over the timer?"

Grumann's hand tightened upon the doorknob as the speaker paused.

"Stan said we had to synchronize the three nuclear explosions. To magnify the destruction."

The security officer knew there were four men on the other side and couldn't speculate on the fate of his ship. He had no control over that. But what he did have was sixteen rounds in his 9mm firearm. With the element of surprise, Grumann could kill or subdue the perpetrators.

He took a deep breath and twisted the doorknob. Just before he entered, the same man who had been talking, coughed. "Teams one and three will be back in a few minutes. So, it shouldn't matter if our explosion went off early. Even if it did, we don't have to tell Stan."

Grumann slowly released the knob.

Did the math.

Three teams of four each.

Twelve bullets to do the job.

Sixteen left in his gun.

With odds like that, he could win every time.

Unless something went wrong.

45

WRECK AND THE SHRIEKER

BACK IN THE SMALL ANTEROOM, teams one and two had exited with their mini-nukes to start chaos and mayhem upon the sixth alternate planet. Thirty seconds later, the third crew left to complete their mission.

Four determined men carried a two-hundred-pound atomic weapon cradled upon two nylon straps. Wreck, who channeled the persona for his sock puppet, Shrieker, stepped over the dimensional door's threshold onto the downward sloping mining tunnel.

Before the team's departure, Stan had explained that the alternate California mining tunnel was the deepest in the U.S., reaching almost nine thousand feet. This part of the West Coast was notorious for earthquake activity, and the detonation of the nuke would fracture the uneasy balance of underlying tectonic plates. Creating a synergistic effect from the other two exploding nukes, it would quickly escalate destructive earthquakes.

Wreck got his nickname from a popular cartoon character—an oversized, good-natured buffoon with megaphone-like ears whom he unfortunately resembled.

The second part of Wreck's name came from the loud and crude vocalizations of his alter ego, Shrieker, the sock puppet.

Shrieker, a size thirteen men's gym sock, had two black button eyes, a pearl for a nose, and a zipper for lips.

Wreck channeled Shrieker in true third person, Texas titty-twisting, trash-talking style. He did it loud and proud, performed in bold, angry caps, strong enough to offend everyone within spitting distance.

Wreck and the other three crew members illuminated the tunnel with their four helmet lights and soon stopped at the end of the mining shaft.

The hand sock's puppet mouth moved while Wreck delivered the message, *"Shrieker tells MORONS. Put the fucking bomb down."*

Pointing their headlamps at the barren dirt, the team gently lowered the weapon to the ground.

Always curious about his environment, Wreck estimated the surface temperature at the mine's entrance was 80 degrees. Now, with a glance at his iPhone, the temperature app read a sweltering 100 degrees at the bottom of the nine-thousand-foot shaft. He wondered how close to Hell he was, and if Stan ever boosted the heat on his compound's jacuzzi to remind him of home.

Wreck worked the sock puppet's mouth. *"IDIOTS will set the timer!"*

The other men were used to Shrieker's demeaning commands. When they were all back in lockup, the sock puppet persona had purchased their loyalty with plenty of "soups." Prison slang for freeze-dried Ramen noodles.

Even though the escaped convicts were now members of the "free world," their compensation for obeying Shrieker's trash talk was still measured in prison commissary food. The three felons felt they were shrewd businessmen when they renegotiated the payoff of three "soups" a day to the current rate of four packages of Ramen noodles.

Every other day.

What had cost Shrieker seventy-five cents a day in the slammer now rose to a buck outside the prison's razor-wire perimeter.

Every two days.

THE SOCK PUPPET PERSONALITY, WHO verbalized his thoughts through Wreck, was fond of Buddha and attributed him with the saying, *"When the student is ready, the teacher will be there."* In the case of these three nitwit students, Shrieker felt the master had binged with internet porn and beer that day, rather than teach simple math to the mental midgets.

HONORING SHRIEKER'S LAST COMMAND, WRECK waited as one nincompoop bent down and set the timer to thirty minutes. The man rose and joined the group in a quick walk back to the dimensional door.

The four-team members stood before the entrance.

Still speaking for the puppet, Wreck furiously worked his sock-covered hand while spittle flew from his mouth. *"Three FOOLS always trust Shrieker."*

The team members shifted from foot to foot, waiting for the final message.

"THREE HALFWITS MUST NEVER TRUST STAN!"

Wreck lowered his puppet hand as he severed his mental connection with Shrieker. Because of these words of wisdom, the team of stooges reentered the dimensional door with less enthusiasm than when they'd exited.

He knew each man was promised a cool million from Stan for assaulting the four worlds. And a million dollars would buy them a whole lot of "soups."

Wreck acknowledged the overpowering scent of fear that

strafed the small village of idiots. And admitted that anyone with half a brain would have run.

46

A MESSENGER NAMED DESPAIR

LEE KALE HUNKERED DOWN BEHIND the steering wheel of his '78, baby shit green Gremlin, setting on the edge of the Clements Unit's employee parking lot. Yesterday, he'd discovered the release date for Jason Blaine's money man, Morgan Fairview III. And, today, with a little luck, Lee would follow him back to his boss.

Lee had done his legwork by making sure he didn't park in the lot's surveillance camera range. And last night he'd called in sick, installed a small video cam on the Gremlin's dash, and loaded his .38 Special with high-velocity bullets.

He had linked the dime-sized dash cam to his cell phone, which actively fed into the cloud, assuring that if something bad happened to him, the authorities would have the full story. In the event of his death, Lee had also left a detailed letter about his involvement in Jason Blaine's escape. The note divulged Lee's "loan" and the subsequent coercion which forced him to help the felon escape.

He patted the revolver tucked inside his coat pocket and glanced at his watch.

4:10 p.m.

Fairview would be escorted out by two prison guards any minute now.

4:15 p.m.

Five rows away a dark Lincoln Continental with blacked out windows pulled into the visitor's spot in front of the prison's security entrance.

Peering between rows of parked cars, Lee gripped his cracked steering wheel and took a shaky breath. What he was about to do was illegal, immoral, and totally insane. But, two lives were in jeopardy—his infant son and his own. Unfortunately, his bitchy divorced wife wasn't in the gun's crosshairs.

Lee looked at his watch again, glanced up, and bit his lip. On the walkway between the prison and the razor-wired perimeter fence were two guards escorting the man he recognized as Morgan Fairview III.

Blaine's money man was unblemished from ten years in prison. Tall and rugged looking with lightly grayed hair at the temples, the rest of his mane was jet-black, cut short, and spiked on top.

While Fairview sauntered down the concrete path, he engaged the officers in banter, eliciting laughter from both men.

The trio paused at the perimeter gate, then passed through the entry point when the electronic lock snicked back.

From his vantage point twenty yards away, Lee watched the men enter the cinder block security station. It was the last checkpoint blocking Fairview's freedom. And once he'd exited, Lee knew it marked the beginning of a new life for the felon who'd refused to betray his friend and master, Jason Blaine.

Because he couldn't afford to replace his car's broken ignition switch, Lee had to hotwire it and prayed that it would start. He pinched two wires together, the motor shuddered to life, and Lee took a grateful breath as Morgan Fairview III strutted out of the security post, directly to the waiting Continental.

The limo driver exited, opened the passenger door for Fairview, closed it for him, then settled back behind the wheel. A moment later, the chauffeur backed out of the visitor's spot.

Lee watched the departing vehicle, put his foot on the brake, and shifted into reverse.

Just before he hit the accelerator, cold steel entered the open window and touched his temple. Lee jerked in horror. He turned to his left. Saw the smirk on Jason Blaine's face as the escaped felon cocked his weapon.

"Hey, Mailman." Blaine tapped Lee's shoulder with his weapon. "Let's take a drive. We need to talk."

Lee white-knuckled the steering wheel. The inside of his mouth turned desert dry. His heart cycled at the speed of light, just a photon away from stroking out. He closed his eyes. Prayed for his son—a child who, at best, could become fatherless and, at worst, murdered by a psychotic killer.

Lee Kale choked on the bitter tang of guilt as Blaine squeezed in the back seat of the two-door Gremlin.

The killer pointed his pistol at the nape of Lee's neck. "I assume you brought a gun. So, hand it over."

Lee slowly removed it and passed his gun to Blaine.

"I get the feeling you came to kill me. Someone's gonna die today, and it sure ain't me." Blaine rolled his eyes then grinned. "Bet you wonder how I knew you'd be here?"

A Texas-sized lump of fear wedged in Lee's throat, and he choked on a mouthful of shock and dismay. "How?"

"The same way I knew you came armed. The same way I knew you left a letter to the authorities. The same way I knew you put in a dash cam. If you haven't figured it out yet, shithead, it's the same thing I woulda done."

Jason Blaine lowered his automatic. "Your video cam, your letter, your gun can't save your fucked-up life. And I hope you kissed your baby goodbye this morning cause your best efforts won't save his life, either."

Lee's ears roared, and his eyesight blurred. His heart hurled up his throat, and a blood vein burst in his nose.

Blood slowly trickled down Lee's upper lip.

Dribbled across his lips. Dropped from his chin.

He hung his head and cried. Cried for how he had failed his son.

"You are so fucked, Mailman." Jason Blaine motioned with his gun for Lee to drive.

Before Lee could back out, the passenger door opened, and a hideously disfigured woman scooted into the back seat, shoved her skateboard on the floorboard, and grinned like a fiend from Hell.

Lee's face twisted in horror when he looked at her face and neck. Covered with black, cancerous patches, her exposed skin looked like burnt marshmallow. The woman's blizzard white hair and warped knuckles screamed advanced age. And with a spine twisted from bone disease, she resembled the specter of Death.

She reached over and touched Blaine's bare arm.

Blaine jerked backward, and his face warped from disgust and revulsion. He leveled the gun at her forehead. "Who the hell are you?"

"I'm the messenger of death. But you can call me Despair."

Jason Blaine overcame his revulsion, winked at Despair, and shifted his game into overdrive. "What's on your mind, sweetheart?"

"I'm an empath, and from the touch of your arm, I know things about you."

"Please, tell me more."

"You want to overthrow Satan."

"Yep." Blaine chuckled.

"You want to rule Hell."

"Damn straight." The convict leaned closer.

Despair moved her lips, exposing decayed and missing teeth. "Then I've got a deal you can't refuse."

Blaine punched the back of Lee's neck. "You hear that, Mailman? I've got a deal to cut, so put this piece of shit car in gear. And drive."

47

NAKED AND AFRAID

INSIDE A DARK CAVERN, GRUMANN, the cruise boat security chief, glanced at the glowing hands of his watch. Still hunkered behind the door that had just admitted four men, he accepted the fact that they had destroyed his cruise ship with a high-powered bomb. Possibly a mini-nuke. And from the conversation he'd overheard earlier, there would be three teams of four men each meeting up in the next room. Judging from the number of voices coming through the door jamb, Grumann was confident that everyone had set the timers on their bombs and returned.

If the perpetrators of this horrible crime succeeded, the metropolis he called home could already be destroyed by massive earthquakes.

His hands trembled as he unbuttoned his collar. He was stranded inside a mysterious chamber and couldn't make sense of anything since he'd entered the ship's broom closet. And then the disturbing scuttle and click of claws upon stone moved toward him in the dark. Unable to see, he could still smell and recognized the stench of decaying flesh. From the sweet and rotten odor, it was too damn close for comfort.

Distant whispers drilled through the dark, and he caught a few words.

"Fresh meat... hunger... kill."

A pounding migraine started in his temple and shot to the back of his head. Something out there had an appetite for human flesh, and he had no desire to be today's entrée. Whatever this freakshow was, he had to get the hell out of here.

And soon.

Grumann still had his ear against the door, and when the muffled conversation in the next room ended, it was time to make his move.

He checked the hammer of his Beretta 9mm, made sure it was cocked, and took a deep breath. Swinging the door open, he stepped into a small, semicircular anteroom.

Overhead fluorescent lights illuminated a long back wall and three steel doors that were spaced evenly in the curved half.

Twelve surprised faces stared at him. To generate shock and awe, he swung the barrel of his 9mm from one head to the next.

He licked the sweat off his upper lip. "Think twice before you do anything rash. Because my mood really sucks, and I'm a breath away from pulling the trigger."

Within spitting distance from the men, Grumann steadied his gun. "There are twelve of you. And one of me. I have enough bullets for each man and can hit a two-inch target at fifteen feet." He looked each person in the eye and shrugged. "If you think you can overpower me, most, if not all of you, will die. Today, the only question you should ask yourself is, are you faster than a bullet?"

The stink of nervous sweat filled the room as the men calculated the odds. In a few moments, each one nodded in acquiescence. Grumann had won.

"Now, gentlemen, I'm giving you a chance to live." He gestured with his gun. "But you will *not* pass Go. Nor will you collect two hundred dollars. Now strip and move your sorry asses through door two."

His command to disrobe was meant to intimidate as well as reveal any hidden weapons.

The men moved slowly, self-consciously, reluctantly removing a piece at a time.

Just as the last man finished, Grumann caught a telling movement at the back of the anteroom.

An incongruous motion.

A small dark object.

Aimed at his chest.

A microsecond passed. Grumann narrowed his profile. Leveled his gun. Squeezed the trigger. Within the small enclosure, thunder roared. A jagged flame shot from his muzzle. And a bullet exploded the opposing shooter's head.

The sharp burn of cordite and the scent of fresh blood filled the air.

Startled and stunned, eleven nude men scrambled, clawed, and stumbled over each other to get away from the dead man. Grumann calmly walked through the retreating mass, retrieved the gunman's weapon, and put it in his waistband.

"Anyone else?" He waved his gun. "Plenty of ammo left."

The naked men averted their eyes.

"Good. Now file through this door."

They shuffled past Grumann, sullen and stonily, with heads turned downward. After the last man entered, he shut the steel door, turned the deadbolt, and locked them inside.

Placing his ear against the crack between the frame and door, he listened to the men's curses.

"What the hell's that noise?" The speaker, on the other side, was breathy, desperate, and frightened.

The man's fear brought a grin to Grumann's face.

A beat ensued. And he remembered the click and scuttle of claws upon the floor while inside the cavern. Grumann was counting on the faceless monsters behind the steel door to lead the pigs to slaughter.

Then the security chief heard the same words spoken to him earlier in the dark.

Only this time, there were more voices, and they weren't whispering. An ungodly screech assaulted his ears. A chorus of ghouls chanted, *"FRESH MEAT... HUNGER... KILL!"*

The first victim's scream was high-pitched and twisted from the horrible pain. It aborted into a deep guttural moan. Then, ten other men shrieked. An electric charge shot up Grumann's spine. Their terror ripped through his heart.

Even amidst the horror, he experienced a sense of western justice. A sublime feeling of completion. He looked at his watch again. Thirty minutes were gone. All the bombs had ignited. Earthquakes were beginning, and his world was so fucked.

But now it was Grumann's time. Time for vengeance. The deaths of these men wouldn't compensate for the slaughter of innocent civilians. Because there was a mastermind behind the attack, and while he could still draw a breath, he would hunt the perpetrator down, draw and quarter him, then urinate on the remains.

Grumann turned away from the steel doors in the semi-circular anteroom and examined the room's flat back wall. He rubbed his burning eyes with his open palms and blinked. He took a moment to study the barrier, then detected the faint outline of an exit.

His gut told him that wherever this entryway led, it would take him to the source behind all the death and chaos.

Since there was no doorknob, Grumann pushed against the left side of the rectangular outline. Nothing happened. He pressed a bit lower, and the door popped open.

He took a step forward.

Turned to his left.

His jaw dropped.

And Grumann's already strained sense of reality exploded off the page.

48

A PIECE OF HELL

GRUMANN, THE CRUISE SHIP SECURITY chief, stepped from the semicircular anteroom and glanced to the left. Adrenaline hit his nervous system, and he stiffened from shock. Illuminated by overhead fluorescent lights, an infinite number of beige doors extended as far as he could see. Turning to the right, he observed the same sight.

He didn't know where he was or what this hallway represented, and the resulting anxiety shot a penetrating shaft of pain through his brain. Grumann's six-foot frame curled in agony as he rubbed his eyes, then pinched the bridge of his nose. Pushing through the pounding affliction, he forced himself to focus on his surroundings to divert his thoughts. His analytical mind observed the fresh hallway air, yet there was no evidence of circulation. A glance confirmed the absence of ventilation grills anywhere along the walls.

What the hell had he gotten into, and what was this place? His curiosity piqued, he walked to the closest door and cautiously gripped its knob. The frost-covered metal stung his hand as he started to turn the handle.

"I wouldn't do that. You have *no* idea what's on the other side of that door."

The female voice came from behind him, and he cursed

himself for his lapse of attention. Moments ago, the hallway was empty. Now, three young women had entered and stood fifteen feet away. The one who had just spoken was Caucasian. Next to her was an Asian and Hispanic. A monster of a black man loomed behind them, dressed in hooker pink and held the leash of a four-pound Chihuahua—a dog with six-inch dreadlocks and a studded collar that daintily hiked its leg and peed on the floor.

Things had just gone from scantily south of weird to nakedly north of bizarre.

"I'm Archer." The white woman pointed to her three companions. "And this is Jacqui Chen, Luanne Martinez, and Tenkiller."

The trio acknowledged his presence with brief nods.

"My name's Grumann."

From the looks of Archer, she was in her early twenties, obviously pregnant, and blended natural beauty with penetrating blue eyes.

The group moved forward, and she extended her hand. "We're short on time, and my intuition says we might be able to help each other. So, press your palm against mine."

Sensing no danger, Grumann lowered his gun. He was tempted to go back and reopen the door he'd just stepped through. With his livelihood compromised, he had no place to go and certainly didn't want to reenter the cavern with the flesh-eating ghouls.

Grumann had a hunch and always listened to his gut. In this case, his internal voice told him to trust Archer. With total faith, he slipped the 9mm in his holster, moved closer, and pressed his palm against hers.

As he closed his eyes, a mild electric charge traveled up his arm, spawning images and information that exploded within his mind. Vivid pictures revealed Satan masquerading as the innocuous accountant, Stan. Grumann saw the farm where horror smothered the homeless people. People whose harvested blood was being sold as an energy supplement.

He drew a sharp breath when he absorbed the information that six of eight planets within the multiverse had been assaulted over the past few days by Satan.

Because the palm to palm connection with Archer was two-way, he was intimately aware of her role in the opposition of Stan's takeover. Grumann understood her part in the Sisters of Three, as well as being the leader of the female triumvirate.

He was privy to all her information, just as she was to his.

In less than five seconds, the transfer of images and thoughts was complete.

Archer released his hand. "We can use your help to stop Stan's takeover."

Grumann's migraine finally abated. He took a deep breath, fisted his right hand, and shook it. "Count me in. Because I'm ready to kick ass."

He and the newly-formed team paused, then turned when a nearby door opened. Jacqui and Luanne's faces twisted in astonishment when a twenty-something female entered the Hallway of Infinity. The pixie-like woman's hair cascaded in fashionable curls about her slender shoulders. And her inquisitive face held an abundance of childlike innocence.

The young female touched Archer's arm. "I hope you and the new team are ready, because Stan has opened a portal between Earth and your alternate world. And you have less than two hours to crash the connection before the two planets are compromised from disharmonic gravitational vibrations."

Grumann arched an eyebrow.

Archer's lips raised in a smile. "There is an infinite number of doors here in the Hallway of Infinity. And each one opens upon an alternate world. Tara's job is to protect the integrity of the multiverse. With her guidance, the five of us will close Stan's breach of the two worlds."

Archer glanced at Jacqui and Luanne. "You both have family on Earth."

The possibility of losing kin warped their faces with fear.

A tear slowly trickled down Jacqui's face. "My mother and father are there."

Luanne crossed her arms, staring into space. "I have loved ones, too. And we can't let them die."

Tara nodded at Archer. "Six months ago, on Earth, Allen Costas was instrumental in your parents' and boyfriend's deaths. As a result, you stole a permanent induction pill that allowed you to transfer your consciousness to an alternate world with an alternate Archer. The drug has a six-month grace period before it becomes indefinite. Your window to return ends in two hours. So, either stay in this world or go back to Earth before your physical body dies."

Conflicting emotions erupted upon Archer's face, and the underlying message hit home with Grumann. His psychic connection with her filled in the blanks. All was not right in Archer's alternate paradise, which made it imperative to crash the breach and rescue Earth. Not only for Archer's possible return but to save her two friends' families as well.

Tara reached into her pocket and pulled out a palmed-sized pentagon. "It's time to get started. This key will unlock the connection between the two breached worlds."

The protector of the multiverse handed Archer the metallic device. "When you place this in the receptacle at the top of the portal frame, it will sever the connection and return the worlds to their natural order."

Tara motioned for them to follow, then stopped a few yards later. She locked eyes with each team member. "Inside this door is Stan's compound. But heed my warning. In your journey to save the breached planets, each of you will pass through Hell before you reach the light."

49

LET'S MAKE A DEAL

LEE KALE'S HEARTBEAT SPIKED INTO the stroke zone as he stood ramrod straight in front of his '78 Gremlin. The cause of his distress was the gun Jason Blaine aimed at his head.

Fifteen minutes earlier, at Blaine's direction, Lee had parked under a grove of Cottonwood trees directly across from Stan's secluded compound. And now, the car's engine popped as the metal slowly cooled. Dappled sunlight from the wind-blown leaves above played across Lee, Blaine, and Despair's faces. Three diverse people who were thrown together. And together, they had three diverse stories. Lee thought of his role as prison mailman and how he'd helped Jason Blaine escape. Now, all he wanted to do was kill the bastard. Despair, the self-proclaimed messenger of death who had a deal for Blaine. And finally, Blaine, the escaped convict who wanted to take the reins of Hell from Stan. The devil.

During the last quarter-hour, Lee had listened to a mind-bending conversation between his captor and the messenger of death. Despair claimed that her alter-ego, Hope, would follow her spiritual GPS to someone with a terminal illness, lay hands upon them, absorb their disease, and leave. But Hope could only retain so much illness until it was time for her to purge.

Lee recognized a message with a *Twilight Zone* zip code when Despair revealed that Hope would die unless she passed the absorbed diseases on to someone with a heart as black as Hell. If Hope were able to transfer her illnesses, she would go on living. But the recipient would die.

Lee glanced at Despair, who was winding up her pitch to Blaine. "The only way you can take over the reins of Hell is with my help."

Blaine casually stroked his chin with thumb and forefinger. "Let me get this straight. I allow you to dump all the illness in your body. Into mine. And then... I die?"

Lee was officially in the Zone, expected to see Ray Bradbury any minute. His view of reality had nose-dived six feet below normal in the last few moments. Because a female version of Monty Hall was playing a supernatural interpretation of Let's Make a Deal.

The offender snorted. "If I agree to your offer, there's no upside. Because I'd be dead."

Despair gurgled a wet and disturbing sound, and Lee glanced her way. It could have been blood or bile or a ghastly mixture of the two coming from her lungs or stomach with each tortured breath. And even if her pitch to Blaine was all bullshit, Despair's approaching death was already feet, limbs, and torso inside the hurt locker. Lee was dead certain the door was about to slam shut upon her.

The messenger of death recovered her composure and cleared her throat. "Without me, you cannot replace Stan. The ruler of Hell is untouchable by mortals."

"So, you're offering me the chance to take his place if I agree to your terms. And if I do, that means, what?"

"Blaine, here it is, down and dirty. You will absorb seventeen terminal afflictions in my body, then die a quick and painful death."

"How quick?"

Despair glanced at her watch. "Two minutes top."

"How painful?"

The messenger of death grinned. "You don't want to know."

"Try me."

Despair coughed a deep lung death rattle. Then she reached into her mouth and pulled a loose molar from its socket. Threw it onto the dirt below and wiped her bloody fingers on her pant leg.

Lee heard the four-note Twilight Zone intro, do de do do, and choked on his breakfast as it rammed up his throat.

The messenger of death grimaced. "As I said earlier, I have absorbed seventeen illnesses. Seventeen life-ending diseases."

Blaine raised his eyebrows in an unspoken question.

"Don't bother with how I got them. Just focus on what will happen if you agree to my deal. Within seconds of the transfer, your skin will begin to tingle. Then a subcutaneous burning will be followed by painful lesions. In some cases, it can take weeks for skin cancer to spread. Yours will erupt in minutes. Next, comes shortness of breath and then a savage cough as your lungs fill with liquid.

"Internal organs, once young and healthy, will age and putrefy. From the shock and damage to your body, you'll lose control of your bladder and probably shit your pants. And keep in mind, there will be fourteen other illnesses competing for the end of your life."

As the conversation lulled, Lee wondered when Despair would reveal the upside to Blaine's death. He wiped the sweat from his face and glanced to his left at the devil's exclusive countryside digs. A quarter-mile, fifteen-foot barrier encircled the devil's remote compound. Lee desperately prayed Despair would wrap this up and keep Blaine focused on Stan instead of him.

Blaine spat on the dirt below. "For two minutes, I'll suffer extreme agony, die a horrible death, and gain what?"

Lee studied Despair's face. Her skin had turned blacker and

now exuded an oily sheen. Clumps of hair had fallen upon her
shoulders, and she smelled like rotting fish. If she were going
to swing this deal, it would have to be damned quick.

Despair picked at her arm and dug her curved, yellow nail
into the blackened skin. "The one thing you'll gain after the
death of your physical body is immortality. Your astral body
will manifest itself, and only then will you be able to confront
Stan. Without my help, you cannot defeat Satan. Since God
prohibits him from directly killing mortals, he can't terminate
you himself. So, you have an added incentive to accept my offer.
Because he'll either have one of the escaped convicts murder
you, turn you over to the authorities for execution after you're
no longer useful, or something more devious."

Blaine's face turned thoughtful. "Once I become immortal,
then how can I kill Stan?"

Despair coughed, and it sounded like a toilet flushing. "You
don't kill him. You can't destroy an immortal being."

Blaine motioned with his gun. "Okay, cupcake. Wrap it up."

She touched her brow, drawing a deep breath. "When I
transfer my illnesses to you, you will have the opportunity to
pass them along to Stan. And when you do, he will become
weakened. There has never been one continual ruler of Hell.
As a result, usurpers have claimed the title of Satan throughout
history. And the position has always gone to the one with the
blackest heart and the most power."

Despair suddenly gasped. She bent over and hugged her
chest. A stream of blackened blood spewed from her mouth
and ran down her chin. She tried to stop the flow with her
hand, but it gushed across her palm and through her fingers.

Blaine jerked when the spray hit him in the face.

Despair pulled a wad of tissues from her pocket. Wiping the
blood from her face, chest, and hand, she struggled to regain
her self-control. Finally, she extended her clean right hand to
Blaine. "Do we have a deal?"

Lee saw the uncertainty in the offender's eyes, then averted his gaze when Blaine caught him staring.

"I don't believe you." Blaine leveled his gun at Despair. "And I think all this illness transfer is bullshit."

She reached down and tugged at her sagging Jimmy Choo boot. "I'd swear upon the Holy Bible that what I've said is true. Once we get inside, things will take off. And when that happens, it might be too late. Too late to dump my illnesses. Too late to weaken Stan. The next half-hour won't be for the faint-hearted. So, believe the sign over the compound's entrance."

Lee looked up, read the words, and shuddered. Painted in blood, it presented a dire message.

All ye who enter here can kiss their ass goodbye.

His heart pounded. His hands trembled. And his imagination conjured the sound of dirt hitting his coffin lid. In a moment of righteous prayer, Lee promised God that if he lived through this, he would never... ever borrow money again.

50

WHAT'S ON YOUR MIND?

LEE LOCKED EYES ON STAN'S compound, jerked his gaze to Despair, then back to Blaine.

The felon shoved a gun in Lee's face and grinned. "Bet you wonder what I've got planned for you."

His racing mind conjured up the worst-case scenario, which included sharp knives, rusty bone saws, and excruciating agony.

"Mailman, when you showed up at the prison parking lot, I knew you set out this morning to kill me. Your lethal intent will be dealt with harshly, painfully, and ever so slowly. You'll serve as an example to my team that when someone tries to take me out, bad shit follows."

Lee thought of his actions that led to this situation. The loan shark debt and subsequent extortion. A horrifying death threat against his young son. Remorse consumed him, and it felt like a ball of barbed wire lodged in his throat. But he didn't trust his voice, afraid that fear would show through his words, so he glared at the dirt.

"Just what I thought, Mailman. You got no cojones." Blaine pointed at Lee's crotch, then jerked his thumb toward Stan's compound. "You and the bitch put your asses in gear and head up the road."

Despair turned and shuffled down the dirt path like a doddering invalid until she stumbled on a rock. Lee reached over to steady her and realized she was in no shape to walk alone. So, he linked his arm with hers and gently guided her down the rutted road. The trio passed through the gate and trudged up to the compound's massive oak door.

Blood dribbled over Despair's lips as she stopped to rest on the concrete porch. Her lungs gurgled and wheezed for a minute until she caught her breath. Lee released her arm but stayed close by in case she collapsed.

Despair raised her hand to shade her eyes from the afternoon sun, then nodded at Blaine. "I know things about you, Jason."

"You don't know shit." Blaine hammered his fist on the wooden door.

"But I do." Despair spoke softly like she was talking to a child. "From an early age, you've been able to use logic and figure out what's going to happen. Use your gift, Jason. Can you trust Stan? I don't think you can. So, tell me... what's he going to do?"

When Blaine leveled his gun at her, Lee leaped in front of Despair.

"Get your ass out of the way, Mailman, or there'll be two bodies to dispose of."

Lee straightened his shoulders and took a deep breath. He didn't care that the bully was stronger. He didn't care if he took a beating. But he did care about the life of his innocent child. And this time, Lee was ready to take Blaine down. "I've had enough of your threats, asshole. If you want to put the gun down, let's do this man to man. Fist to fist. Just leave her alone.

"What the hell are you so afraid of, Blaine? Some ninety-pound invalid who's trying to help you?" In a moment of insight, Lee realized several things. For whatever reason, the felon didn't have a clue about Stan's agenda, and secondly, Despair needed Blaine to absorb her illnesses to keep her alive. If she were able to drive a wedge between Blaine and Stan, by insinuating potential betrayal, Blaine might agree to the transfer of her terminal diseases.

Lee's body shook from a dangerous cocktail of fear and adrenaline. He clenched his jaw, thought about his one-year-old son, and moved a step closer to Blaine. "Is the big bad convict afraid to listen? Afraid to accept advice? Or is he just afraid?"

On the left side of the massive door, an open window funneled a chorus of angry voices from a distant hallway.

Lee cupped his hand behind his ear. "Listen, Blaine. Someone knows you're here. And it sounds like a shit load of pissed-off people. My gut tells me Stan's sent them. I'd bet they're coming for you."

Despair cut her eyes toward Lee, and he knew they both wanted the same results. Turn Blaine against Stan, transfer Despair's illnesses, then escape the compound alive.

Lee realized that if he could kill Blaine after Despair downloaded her illnesses, then he would never have to fear the felon.

Lee gritted his teeth. "Use your fucking mind. Tell me what Stan has planned."

With his gun still on Lee, Blaine's lips curled. "Don't screw with me, Mailman. And don't ever tell me what to do."

Lee turned his palms up in an earnest plea. "Don't you realize you can't trust the devil? Do you think he gets happy face reviews from the people he's fucked over? He's Satan. That's what he does. So, for God's sake, use your freakin' logic. Tell us what he plans to do to you."

Blaine lowered his weapon, wiped the sweat from his brow. "All right. I know what Stan's gonna do. And it's fucking nothing."

From the look on the felon's face, Lee knew Blaine was lying.

Lee put his arm around Despair, and she leaned against him for support. Her lungs heaved, labored for oxygen, and he didn't have to be psychic to know her body was shutting down. The voices from the hallway drew closer, and Lee had an uneasy feeling.

In the distance, birds chirped, and a brisk Texas breeze rustled the Cottonwood's leaves. The compound's Lone Star flag snapped and popped in the wind as its metal fittings clanked against the flagpole.

Lee recognized the faint *kerthunk* of a bullet being chambered. He looked over Blaine's shoulder at the compound gate.

A man in black aimed a rifle at them.

The slug ripped through Blaine's right shoulder and exited his chest.

A millisecond later, Lee heard the explosion.

He jerked away as the victim collapsed on the concrete porch. The two men and Despair were safely hidden behind a three-foot stone wall while Blaine clutched the exit wound on his right chest. He blinked as blood trickled from his body. Frothy red bubbles oozed across his lips, down his chin, and puddled on the concrete. He motioned Lee closer. Gripping his arm, Blaine pulled him down until their faces nearly touched. "She's right… Stan had me shot. Tell Despair, I'll… accept her illnesses."

Blaine closed his eyes and choked on a mouthful of blood. "Do it. Before I die."

51

THE HURT LOCKER

THE STEEL DOOR SLAMMED SHUT, and the fine hairs on Lee's neck rose when the outside lock slid into place. He, Despair, and the dying Blaine found themselves imprisoned in a concrete holding cell just off the media room in Stan's compound.

After Blaine was shot, the devil's team of escaped convicts had drug them to the ten by twenty room. Painted in prison grey, the cell had no toilet or bunk. What looked like faint blood stains covered the floor. The stench of death clung to the cell-like stink on shit. Despair hung her head in exhaustion, leaning against the back wall while blood leaked from her eyes and ears. Ten feet away, Blaine lay on the floor, bleeding out from a chest wound. Lee reached into his pocket and removed a clean linen handkerchief. He bent down and pressed it against the exit wound on Blaine's chest.

Lee wanted to kill the fucking psychopath. And the sooner, the better. But he had the overpowering urge to keep him alive, to wait until Despair could do her transfer. The feeling resonated on a deep spiritual level, and Lee knew better than to ignore it. For now, this was the right thing to do. He glanced down at Blaine. "Keep pressure on the cloth to stop the bleeding."

A frothy mass of red bubbled over Blaine's lips and dribbled down the side of his face. He opened his eyes and rolled his head to the right, allowing the blood to drain from his mouth. "Mailman… get her. I'm ready."

Closer to death than life, Despair shuffled across the cell. She stopped next to Blaine and slowly kneeled, gently brushed the hair from his forehead, then placed her hands against each side of his head.

She swayed, and Lee reached out to steady her. Always one to calculate the odds, it was a crap shoot as to whether Blaine or Despair would die first.

Despair sniffled as blood trickled from her nose. "Do you, Jason Blaine, agree to accept all my illnesses, knowing that you will die a painful death?"

Blaine clutched the cloth tighter. "Yes… I…." A heavy cough wracked his lungs, and blood bubbled around the corners of his compress. "Agree."

"Then, with the power of darkness and misery, I condemn your physical body to an excruciating death."

The color drained from Blaine's face, his eyes rolled back, and the felon's legs and arms began to twitch.

An alarming drop in temperature caused Lee's exhalation to turn icy white. And Blaine's blood upon the floor began to freeze from the supernatural cold.

A vortex of energized wind birthed itself over Blaine's head, swirled slowly, then gained momentum as Despair held her hands in place.

She turned her face upward and closed her eyes. "From the realm of darkness, open the channel. Allow your servant to purge her impurities into this willing vessel."

The biting, frigid wind brought tears to Lee's face, his nose and fingers throbbed incessantly, and he shivered uncontrollably. The situation moved south of strange when Lee heard the frightening pop of bones as Despair's arthritic back begin to straighten. Moments later, her black, cancerous skin lost its oily sheen.

The whirlwind exploded around them, growing even stronger. The breath was sucked from Lee's throat by the icy maelstrom. His tears froze upon his cheeks.

Circling the edge of the raging wind, Lee heard the screeching of a hundred demons whose horrid cries birthed the sound of evil joy.

Despair turned her eyes upward. "Cast out the illness taken by God's servant, Hope, I say in the name of that which is holy. And place it within this willing body."

Despair maintained her grip upon the side of Blaine's head while his body shook like a sinner on Judgement Day.

The icy wind churned around them, and Lee's eyes opened wide in horror. Blaine's exposed skin mottled with red and grey streaks, then turned sickly yellow. Within a few seconds, black cancerous growths covered his arms, face, and neck.

When Lee glanced at Despair, he involuntarily sucked in the frigid air. Her cancerous skin was healthy and blemish free. And her once white hair now a lustrous black. What had been a decrepit female just minutes ago had turned into a young, vibrant woman.

She maintained her hold on Blaine's head as his spine begin to warp—forcing him into a fetal position.

The felon moaned. Then his moan escalated to a shriek. He kicked at the air, his body writhing from extreme agony.

Despair held her hands in place as Blaine shuddered, his six-foot frame now shriveled and consumed with the seventeen fatal diseases.

Lee blew warm air upon his fingers and noticed the sudden quiet. Gone were the tortured demon's voices and the swirling vortex birthed by Despair.

Blaine's decrepit body quivered once.

Lee glanced over at Despair. "Is it done?"

Her face pinched in uncertainty. "Unless he comes to for the final transition, I'm totally screwed."

"Meaning?"

"He has to be conscious after he receives my diseases. Otherwise, we both die."

52

A GOOD CRY

STANDING IN THE HALLWAY OF Infinity, I grip the knob on the door to Stan's compound. With a glance over my shoulder at the team, I silently absorb the concern on their faces. Luanne and Jacqui meet my gaze as well as Tenkiller and Grumann. Even though no one shows open fear, I detect tension from their rapid breath, nervous sweat, and taut muscles. My stress meter pegs in the red zone, but I hide it well.

Tara the Traveler steps aside and fans her hand at us. "Archer, I'm leaving you now but will pass on a warning. Each of you shall journey through Hell and be exposed to its temptations. So, to your own heart be true."

The team members turn away from Tara and follow me through the door into a plush home theatre room. Three rows of high-end recliners sit in front of a large, blank movie screen. Seated on the first row, reading his book, I recognize Stan from his white button-down dress shirt, black polyester pants, and pocket protector with pens and pencils. And rounding out the definition of geekdom is the fashion statement made by his black horn-rimmed glasses.

Finishing his book, Stan's whimpers engulf us as we approach from behind.

The devil has an empty box of Kleenex on the recliner's

armrest, along with four or five wadded up tissues. As he wipes away a tear and closes the paperback, I'm close enough to read the author and title—Linda Broday and *The Reluctant Ranger.*

I clear my throat, and Stan whips around. "Never had you pegged as a historical romance reader. But I guess everyone can use a good cry."

Stan blushes and quickly wipes the tears away. He crams the romance novel in the crack between the recliners, blows his nose, and jumps up from his seat.

The devil is a head shorter than me and looks up to meet my eyes.

"From all the press I've heard about Satan, I'd imagined you taller and not so… nerdish?"

He puffs up with a quick breath and gains an inch from better posture but still has to look up at me.

Stan sweeps his arm in a grand gesture, bowing slightly. "Let me guess. From the mouth on you, you're Archer. And these two young ladies are Jacqui and Luanne. The tall gentleman to your right wearing the devastating pink outfit must be Tenkiller.

"The last of our guests is Grumann, a cruise ship officer from one of the assaulted worlds."

A tiny bark echoes across the room, and Stan chuckles. "Last, and not least, is Rambo."

After the shock of him knowing our names passes, I'm level with Stan and can look him in the eye. I have the strange feeling that he has somehow grown in the past few minutes. When I note the slope of the media room floor, I write it off that he has moved toward me and only appears taller.

"Now, Archer, I know you and your friends have come to save the last two planets. And as the scenario goes, I will do everything in my power to stop you. So, step up and give it your best."

Stan presses the remote button in his right hand, and the ten by twenty-foot movie screen retracts into the ceiling and reveals a round, seven-foot windowless opening behind it that connects two worlds.

Both planets are held together by a six-inch-wide segment that pulses with a greenish hue. At the top of the arch is the hexagonal insert for the planet releasing key I hold. As I peer across the opening, horror rocks my mind and sucks the energy from my body. The blood rushes from my limbs as I look through this portal. I see my body being tended to in a hospital. The same body I left behind so my consciousness could attach to another Archer on an alternate planet. A portal now connects Earth and my adopted world.

And according to Tara's timeline, both planets will be compromised within thirty minutes.

53

THE OUIJA BOARDS

I'VE GOT A BAD FEELING where this is going. My team and I are in Stan's media room with a dozen recliners, a hidden romance novel, and a large circular opening connecting Earth and my adopted planet. Knowing that the disharmonic gravitational force between the two worlds will destroy them in thirty minutes only reinforces my intuition. The pit of my stomach clenches up because I damn sure don't like where this is going.

Stan snaps his fingers, and an eerie light begins to brighten. The glare emanates from the floor and ceiling, spreading up all four walls—a radiance that imprints the image of hundreds of Ouija Boards across every inch of the room. The basic elements of the board, its black letters and numbers, channel a dark evil aura that feeds and amplifies Stan's energy.

Sometimes called the devil's portal, I know the appearance of the Ouija Boards could be an ugly cancer waiting to consume the team and me.

A glance at Stan reveals his confident body language—fingertips steepled, head tilted slightly. His underlying arrogance also transmits smugness. I don't need an interpreter to know that we are in trouble.

The devil doesn't waste a heartbeat on his message, either.

"Tenkiller." Stan approaches the angel with a gleam in his

eye. "An interesting name. No doubt I'll touch upon the story behind it."

Stan somehow appears taller, and I glance at the cuffs of his pants and see flesh where none showed before.

The devil narrows his profile and cuts his eyes to Ten. "You have a history of self-destructive behavior, don't you? A form of emotional and physical flagellation for the deaths of ten family members. Hence the name, Tenkiller."

The fallen angel squirms and wipes his suddenly moist forehead with the back of his hand.

With his prey firmly in the imaginary crosshairs, Stan applies pressure to the trigger. "The booze and drugs and sex offer refuge from your pain. They help you create a safe place. A place that provides the emotional protection of a warm blanket and a cuddly puppy. A place that castrates the phallus of guilt."

I watch a confident Stan step toward a shaking Tenkiller. He glides across the glowing Ouija Boards and with each step absorbs dark energy from the tainted numbers and letters. The devil places his hand on Ten's arm. "Your God has done nothing to help you."

My heart breaks for the angel when he turns his head in shame. A tear releases and slowly rolls down his face.

The devil pats the side of Tenkiller's cheek. "What the Almighty has done to you, I can undo. I, and I alone. But you must trust me."

The hair rises on the back of my neck when Satan slithers his way to Jacqui and Luanne.

The devil's face is a beacon of concern. "Jacqui, wouldn't you say trust is essential?"

She flips her long black hair back and steps away from him.

As an empath, it's clear to me that Jacqui anticipates Stan's message. Like Tenkiller, she too has suffered loss, deep and personal. I sense her emotional aura thrumming with hope yet tempered by fear.

Stan winks at Jacqui. "If you trust in me, I can bring your twin sister, Christine, back."

Jacqui takes a quick breath. "How? She's been dead for years."

"I can do what your God refuses to do. By the power given to me when He banished me from Heaven."

Stan smiles at Jacqui and leaves her to digest his offer.

He reaches over and brushes the hair from Luanne's forehead. "I know your pain, that hollow emptiness in your gut over the abortion. How many times have you cried from your decision?" Stan puts his forefinger under Luanne's chin and lifts gently. If you trust in me, I will give you back the little girl you long to love."

Luanne clasps her hands across her mouth. As I watch her eyes close, her body shakes from intimate pain.

She whispers through her fingers, "I would give my life to have my baby back."

From where I stand, Grumann has been stonily silent and stares at Stan. The security officer's eyes are wide, and his pupils dilate from powerful emotion.

"Can you bring back my wife, Mary?"

The devil smiles warmly. "The woman who died in your arms after you crashed the car? I can bring her back. And when I do, it will wipe away the guilt and remorse. It will end your migraines. And I will do what God refuses to do. I will make you whole again."

Stan now locks eyes with mine, his smile one of helpfulness. A thousand thoughts rush through my mind. They sprinkle my deepest desire with hope and shower the barren earth of loss with the promise of truth.

"Archer, you have connected with your alternate parents and boyfriend in this parallel world. But I can offer you two things. First, the truth behind who murdered your birth mother and father. And secondly, I know you fear being alone and will restore the integrity of Earth and your alternate planet."

Stan spreads his arms to encompass the team and me. "I will give you all redemption from your errors. Can absolve your guilt and suffering. All you need to do is… trust me."

My internal voice tells me to bolt. Nothing about Stan is good. And even though trusting him is a desperate act, I would trade my soul to know the truth behind my parents' deaths.

Horror and fascination copulate in my gut and spawn squirming larvae that gorge upon my resistance. Resistance that lessens as my friends raise their hands, one by one, in affirmation. I scream internally, *runrunrun,* Yet, the words form in my throat. "I… do…."

Stan stands before me, and now I look up at him.

"You do, *what,* Archer?"

"I… do *not* trust you."

Satan bows his head and raises his arms. A mighty thunderclap explodes inside the media room. Hundreds of Ouija Boards pulse demonic energy through the air. The stink of sulfur stings my nostrils. And the screech of lost souls violates my ears.

But worst of all is Stan's transition.

The monster inside rips through the outer husk of the harmless accountant and slowly reveals the hideous creature within—a demon who is now seven feet tall. Stan's clothes lay in pieces upon the floor as the devil reveals its true self. The ghoul's skin is thick and crusty, connected like jigsaw pieces of broken slate, and oozes a pus-colored slime. Spiny thorns push through the hard-exterior twisting with demonic force until they reach six inches in length.

The demon towers above us, an ungodly agent bent on death and destruction. It has no lips yet forces its words clearly and concisely, "Four of you have chosen. And now, I am your God. Kneel and worship before your new master."

An unholy shriek rises above the din of discarnate voices around us, strafes my ears, ignites my terror.

Horrified… I realize the scream is mine!

FALLING APART

LEE KALE WANTED TO KILL the psychopath, Jason Blaine, but ironically chose to try to save the asshole's life. The spiritual insight received earlier about keeping Blaine alive was still in place. But running close behind was the option to let the Nazi trash die.

Still locked in the holding cell with a rejuvenated Hope, Lee knelt beside the unresponsive Blaine. Shook his shoulder. "Hey, are you all right?"

Hope positioned herself across from Lee. Her brow furrowed with worry when the felon didn't respond. "Check his pulse."

Lee placed two fingers on Blaine's neck, located the carotid artery, then held his breath. Fifteen seconds later, he shook his head no at Hope.

"Can you do CPR?" Her voice rose in alarm.

"Yes, I can." But it grated on him, saving the piece of shit convict who had threatened him and his son's life.

Lee straightened the criminal's body, placed his hands over the lower part of Blaine's sternum, then began a set of fifteen compressions.

Blood bubbled out of the exit wound on Blaine's chest with each downward thrust until Lee stopped to position the head.

Placing his right hand against the felon's jaw and his left

on the top of Blaine's forehead, Lee lifted and tilted until he opened the airway.

He pinched the nostrils shut and reluctantly put his mouth over Blaine's and gave two quick rescue breaths.

Chunks of cancerous flesh sloughed off against his lips, and the taste and smell shocked his senses, triggering a blast of projectile vomit. The bile gushed against Blaine's side and thoroughly covered Lee's thighs.

Undeterred by the smell and horror, Lee continued with the chest compressions and breathing until he finished the final set.

Hope, who had watched closely, leaned forward as Lee checked for a pulse.

His fingers, slick with bile and cancerous skin, were wedged into Blaine's neck.

Seconds passed—still, no pulse.

Lee adjusted his fingers until he relocated the hollow between the windpipe and neck muscles. He pressed again.

Just as he was about to tell Hope it was too late, Lee felt a faint beat. The breath caught in his throat, and he looked up. "I think he's alive."

Amid the puke and blood, Lee and Hope kneeled on either side of Blaine's body watching the deepening inhalations followed by reciprocal exhalations.

The chest wound still gurgled, and the criminal was barely alive. Lee reached down and shook Blaine's shoulders. "Can you hear me?"

Jason Blaine slowly opened his eyes, coughed deep within his chest, then spit blood onto the concrete floor.

Hope leaned over so the felon could see her. "There's not much time. So, Jason, now that you have received all my illnesses, do you accept your coming death?"

His eyes rolled back, and he took a shallow breath.

This time Lee shook his shoulders harder. "Damn it, stay with us, Blaine."

The convict's body trembled, and he blinked several times. After a moment, the tremors subsided, and he reached up to touch Lee's cheek.

"Es fine."

Hope's face twisted with urgency. "Jason, for this to work, I need you to say, 'I agree.'"

"I...." Jason Blaine choked on his blood, twisted his body in pain, before answering, "I... agree."

Lee Kale leaned back and looked at Hope.

She returned his gaze and answered his unspoken question of what happens next? "Now, we wait."

The dying Blaine gave up a profound death rattle and curled into a fetal position.

Hope's gaze never left the felon's face. "It won't be long now."

Lee sensed the moment Blaine died, felt a heavy pressure lift from his body and mind. Now, he was free. Free to live again. A liberation that meant he was ready to get a new job, far away from the prison and all its trouble and turmoil.

But as quickly as the veil of fear lifted, a brutal realization stopped Lee cold. If Blaine usurped Satan, would he come after Lee and his son when he became the ruler of Hell?

Hope stood and extended her gloved hand to Lee as he rose. She gave him an enigmatic smile. God knows your concerns, Lee. So, trust in Him."

Even with the eerie timing of her comment, what other choice did he have? So, he took Hope's gloved hand, and together they watched Jason Blaine's astral body emerge from his earthly corpse.

There was a sucking sound as Blaine separated from his physical shell. His transparent body rose until he stood before them, still retaining the cancerous skin, deeply congested lungs, along with the leaking chest wound.

All seventeen illnesses were still in place as the newly dead felon fist pumped the air. "To quote the immortal James Brown,

I feel good." Blaine did a quick two-step shuffle and bowed. "No. I feel better than good. I feel fucking *great*. Now tell me how to take the devil down."

55

HELL ON WHEELS

"AND THAT'S ALL I DO?" Jason Blaine spread his hands toward the cell's wall and knew his incredulity showed. But this was just too bizarre to believe. "You just want me to walk through concrete and rebar, into the media room, and funnel seventeen illnesses to the devil." He gave a roughish grin and wink to Hope.

Hope brushed her thick, black hair away, glanced at Lee Kale, then back at Blaine. "Jason, you're dead, and your astral body works in another realm. And yes, you can pass through walls.

So, when you confront Satan, focus on your anger. Dredge up every ounce of wrath within. Remember all the pain you've encountered in your life. Then multiply it by one hundred. That's the only way you'll defeat him. You've got to drench him in all the negativity you can summon. Suffocate the devil with your fury. Ram your rage down his throat until he drowns on your darkness.

"Once you breach his defenses, extend your hands and channel the illnesses into Satan's body. Overwhelm him with your diseases. To become the next ruler of Hell, you've gotta weaken him into submission. Then you can lay claim to the blackest heart in all of Hades."

Blaine rubbed his hands together and chuckled. "Well, then let's git this sumbitch on the road."

BLAINE TOOK A DEEP BREATH, walked up to the concrete wall, and paused before stepping through the steel reinforced material. A quick stride took him inside the barrier where he encountered no resistance. So, he paced confidently through the solid substance and exited in the media room where he saw three women, two men, a dog, and the devil himself. Every square foot of the room shimmered with the Ouija Board imprint as Blaine charged across the floor.

He stopped ten feet from the devil, extended both arms, and closed his eyes. Then he dredged the darkest part of his tortured soul, freed the depravity that marked his life, and ignited the memory of malevolence and cruelty that nurtured his hatred.

The floor trembled, and Blaine opened his eyes. He had missed Stan's earlier transformation into the seven-foot demon who now bowed his head, clenched both fists, and hissed at him. But he knew the devil's smell, as accountant or demon. The peculiar scent was a shade shy of baby shit and had all the olfactory tags of Satan.

The small audience of five backed up against the far wall, watching him with frightened expressions.

Blaine had never felt so good, so powerful. He escalated his anger and tapped into a fearsome reservoir of dark and evil deeds. The floor that once trembled now shook. And the devil before him clutched his head, bent over in pain.

Blaine tightened his hands and imagined squeezing Satan's neck like a steel vise, cutting off all his air.

The devil hissed and writhed, thrashing against Blaine's invisible grip.

"Had enough, asshole?" Blaine's face lit up with pleasure.

Satan couldn't respond, so Blaine smirked. "Well, hang on, cause you're about to see some really bad shit."

Blaine unclenched his fists, freeing the devil's neck.

Satan gasped for air and took one step toward his adversary. "Don't even think of it."

A massive burst of power exploded through Blaine's hands, took the form of dark energy, and smashed the center of the devil's chest.

The demon screamed in agony. He tried to move but was pinned in place as the fatal illnesses entered his body. Cancer, geriatric spinal warping, terminal COPD were consuming Satan, and still, the onslaught continued, until Blaine purged himself of all disease.

Satan slumped to the ground, whimpered once, and gasped.

Blaine raised his fists in triumph and screamed—a long, piercing note that arced inside the media room, saturating the captive audience of five with its inhumanity, its promise of cruelty, and the soul of insanity.

Satan lay before him, and the kingdom of Hell was Blaine's for the taking.

And then the Ouija Boards turned black. They sucked the light from the room, spawned a soul snuffing darkness, and castrated the remainder of Blaine's joy.

And when Blaine thought things couldn't get any worse.

They did.

56

NOW YOU SEE ME...

SATAN TREMBLED AS HE LAY on the media room's floor. With a shitload of terminal illnesses in his body, he should have been incapacitated, should have lost his power, should have been deposed as ruler of Hell.

In his vocabulary, "shoulda" was a unique word that implied something needed to be done to prevent the possibility of a bad outcome. But as the CEO of Lost Souls, Inc., he was already aware of what would happen today and had promptly applied the six *Ps* of an old military adage—*Prior Planning Prevents Piss Poor Performance.*

The devil knew Jason Blaine had been a willing recipient for the seventeen illnesses. However, Satan also knew he would have them forced on himself. With this prescient information, he had put the Ouija Boards in place to siphon off the dark life-leaching energy. The very nature of the board acted as a communicator with the occult forces by either sending or receiving. The intent of the user determined the process. In Satan's case, he had primed them to receive. And they were doing just that, pulsing around him, drawing the illness from his body.

He slowly got up from the floor and noted Archer and her crew huddled against the far wall deep in conversation. Fully erect now, the seven-foot-tall devil brushed his hand across the six-inch thorns that covered his craggy frame. Then he focused on Blaine's transparent astral body.

"Thought you could replace me, didn't you?" Satan tottered toward Blaine.

Arrogance still flowed off the failed usurper. "Yep, and I almost did."

The devil eyed the convict's face and exposed skin, noting the healthy appearance, now that the illnesses were purged. Always observant, he admired the tattoos, an SS insignia on either side of Blaine's neck, as well as a portrait of Adolf Hitler on his upper chest.

"Jason, you have dedicated decades to your development as a miscreant, consummate criminal, and misanthrope. And from that, you brought death to your competitors, money to your pocket, and gorged yourself on your enemy's fear."

Satan reached out and waved his stone-like hand. "I admire your initiative. The guts it took to try and replace me as ruler of Hell. And you've come the closest to deposing me than all those before you."

The felon straightened with respect and saluted. *"Sieg Heil Mein Fuehrer."*

The gesture was not lost on Satan. "You remind me of my younger days. The drive, manipulation, and deceit are valuable commodities. You've made me proud. And I have a special place in my organization for you."

Blaine's body trembled. He took a shaky breath. "You're not going to destroy my astral body?"

"Of course not. Someone with your deviousness and cunning is meant to be nurtured. And that is why I'm appointing you to my number two position."

The light in the media room finally brightened because the darkened Ouija Boards had extracted the illnesses from Satan's body.

The ruler of Hell nodded affectionately at his new protege.

Jason squirmed with anticipation. "How soon will I be in place?"

"Why, I'll have you up and running after your orientation class." Satan clapped his hands, and Jason Blaine's astral body disappeared. The devil spoke to the space reverently, softly, "Since you're a favorite of mine, I'll expedite the class and see you in a couple of thousand years.

"Until then, burn in the pits of Hell. And hopefully, you'll remember what happens when someone tries to cross me."

Satan projected his voice to Archer and her team, "And now, dear girl, you and I have business to discuss."

I RAISE MY VOICE SO Satan can hear me. "A few days ago, in the Hallway of Infinity, I discovered four alternate worlds that you destroyed. My question is, why? Why did you murder innocent people?"

"Let's get the facts straight, Archer. You just *thought* the planets were destroyed. So, between you and me, I'll share a little secret. Killing all the inhabitants doesn't help me, but having them turn from God *does.*"

Satan reads the confusion upon my face and explains further. "When disasters occur, and death and destruction are rampant, humanity is left wondering how God allowed their loved ones or children to die. The survivors, hearing no answer, condemn their faith and turn from God, which leaves them ripe for my influence. Because a rebellious mind is the devil's workshop. I may destroy cities, even continents, but entire planets, no. I need the survivors of the catastrophes. Without their anger and pain, I have no converts."

I turn my hand's palm up. "Then what about Earth and my alternate world? Are they safe from destruction?"

Satan chuckles and births an evil smile. "In this case, I'm making an exception. Because I want to see the look on your face when they explode."

OMG!

I TAKE A DEFINITIVE STEP toward Satan, who stands in the middle of the media room. To his right is the open portal connecting this alternate world with Earth. A glance at my watch, and I draw a sharp breath. Given the proximity of the two worlds, the planets will explode from disharmonic gravitational vibrations in the next twenty minutes. The hexagonal key, given to me by Tara the Traveler, is slick with sweat from my hand. And for the hundredth time, I wonder when I will be able to use it to release the connected worlds.

My team of two women, two men, and one pint-sized dog follow me across the floor where we form a loose circle around Satan.

I utter two words, *"Prohibere tempus."* It's the phrase I use to stop time.

The devil looms over me. The anxious rasp of my breath and the stress-filled thud of my heart expose the anxiety I fight to control. A glance at the media room wall clock reveals the second-hand gliding smoothly in a circular motion. My team members are unaffected by my command and sway while standing in place. Rambo, Tenkiller's dog, yips and jerks against its leash.

For whatever reason, I can't stop time in the devil's lair. An evil laugh reaffirms that Satan is unaffected by my power.

I instantly focus on his heart, imagine it between two steel jaws, then apply mental pressure, squeeze harder until the flesh bursts, and blood spurts outward.

In my mind, I see the destroyed organ, yet when I look up, Satan is still alive. Alive and pissed off.

"Your pitiful display of psychic power is no match for an immortal being." He exhales, and I gag on his foul breath. "Do you think you can stop me from destroying the last two worlds?" Satan bends down, starts to touch my belly, full with the unborn child, yet stops before making contact. "I can destroy you and your team in the blink of an eye."

Satan gets in Luanne's face. "Do you recall our earlier conversation? The only way to get your unborn baby back is through me."

She spits at his feet. "In a moment of weakness, I believed you. But not any longer."

He moves to Jacqui. "And what about your dead twin sister, Christine? Do you want to see her again?"

"I can't change the past. But Christine will always live in my memories."

The next person in line is Grumann. "You will never touch your beautiful wife again. Can you accept that?"

Grumann looks over at me before speaking. "Mary is dead, and I won't make a deal with the devil. So, screw you!"

Tenkiller stands tall, proudly defiant as the devil confronts him, looks him in the eye, and speaks. "I will release you from your guilt and self-destructive behavior."

"Even though I'm unworthy, a drug and alcohol addict, I will not renounce my God. So, you can take your offer and go to Hell."

Having made his way around the circle and back to me, I know Satan will strike deep within my heart with the question he mentioned earlier.

"Would you like to know who killed your parents, Archer?"

I'd sell my soul to have the answer, but I shake my head no to him. "I don't believe you. What reason do you have to tell the truth?"

"I'll share something with you. To confirm my goodwill."

I tilt my head. "I'll be the judge of that."

"Remember when you and your two friends tried to engage your spiritual, mental, and physical powers at your alternate parents' home?"

"And? Your point is?"

"The point is, your attempt to blend your psychic abilities led you to a sacred, spiritual place, put you before God's Throne. You were but a breath away from the face of God. The aura of His presence had seeped into your soul, layering your consciousness with divine presence. You were before the veil that separates Him from man. Just a heartbeat away from receiving spiritual guidance.

"And then your world crashed around you. Your body fell through blackness so thick, so vile that even the blessed light of God fled from its presence. You plunged into the hideous river of darkness that drug your body to the crushing walls. Walls that obliterate not only the flesh but the soul as well. As you fought against the current, do you remember the harsh shrill voices that strafed your ears?"

Satan mocks me with a slight bow. "'Kill the bitch.' And 'We never wanted you here.'"

I do remember and will never forget the venom, the ultimate hatred behind those words. But I keep my thoughts from showing upon my face.

Satan runs his rock-like hand across the thorns covering his body, which screeches like metal upon metal. "And after you woke from this vision, you thought I was behind it. Didn't you?"

"Well, if it wasn't you, who was it?"

When Satan gets close to my face, waves of evil roll off him. And I sense more revelation to come.

"All journeyers to the Hallway of Infinity are monitored by Tara the Traveler. She interacts with few, but when she does engage, she voices the same warning, 'Those that travel to alternate worlds should know that things are always… a little off.'

"And, Archer, the alternate world you chose to live in with your alternate parents and their pregnant daughter are more than… a little off. The voices you heard were theirs. It was their intent to scare you. It was their desire to run you off. And if that didn't work, it would be their duty to exorcise your spirit from their daughter. Then destroy it."

The devil rumbles with laughter. "You, the astral refugee from Earth, have no place in this alternate world. And your substitute family will eventually kill you to make the point."

My mind jumps back over the past few days and forms a connection. Since my vision with the killing walls, I have not seen or heard from my adopted family or boyfriend. Could there be some truth in Satan's words?

"Join hands." At my command, the team reaches out, grasps palm to palm, and tightens the circle around the devil.

A tingle trickles through my hands, alerting me to rising psychic energy. A glance at my teams' eyes signals their awareness of it, too.

Like we planned when Satan was absorbing the fatal illnesses, I start our offense with a nod to the other two Sisters of the Triumvirate. "Engage your powers, spiritual, physical, and mental. And focus upon the divine within."

We have fifteen minutes to stop the annihilation of two worlds, I may never know if I truly killed my birth parents, and Satan shrieks as a portal of white, spiritual energy cascades over our heads.

58

COLD HEART, HOT FEET

SATAN WRITHES IN AGONY, DROWNING in a waterfall of spiritual light flowing over my four team members and me. Tenkiller, Grumann, Jacqui, Luanne, and I hold hands and encircle the devil while he is separated from us by a circular barrier of holy radiance, which traps him within the center.

The devil hurls his body against the invisible wall, and thunderbolts erupt from the impact. He screeches in rage, smashing his barbed torso against the clear barrier again and again, fracturing off lightning which spews superheated flames—flames that scorch his thorny bristles and desiccated flesh.

I had directed the two Sisters of the Triumvirate to focus upon combining our spiritual, physical, and mental powers. On my left is Luanne, Jacqui to my right. They, in turn, hold Tenkiller's and Grumann's palms. I tighten my grip upon each of my female friends' hands and focus on connecting psychically, willing our effort to invoke Divine intervention.

Fortunately, the other four team members closed their eyes, their consciousness far from this disturbing scene. The hand of God is upon them, flushing their faces with blind ecstasy.

The odor of Satan's burning skin assaults my nostrils, and I choke on the pungent smell. Wisps of smoke rise from his shoulders as he turns toward Grumann.

The seven-foot monster suddenly shimmers like a mirage in the desert. And the devil slowly loses his height, compacting into a smaller shape, which evolves into a middle-aged woman dressed in a powder blue Christian Dior pantsuit with a diamond pendant necklace and matching earrings. A heartbeat later, she frees her pinned-up hair and shakes loose a thick blond mane. The she-devil turns toward Grumann and smiles.

"Lovie, open your eyes. Look at me." Her voice is soft. Sensual. Seductive.

He remains deep in a trance.

"Grummy, it's your wife. Mary."

Like a serpent's tongue, awareness flickers across Grumann's countenance. His eyes flutter open. First shock, then disbelief, and finally astonishment brand their lines upon his face.

"Mary?" The word has the weight of a whisper, yet his underlying love delivers a thunderous roar.

I blink my eyes, swallow once before speaking, then realize I have no voice. My mind screams no, no, no, Grumann! Don't believe him. Don't give in. It's a trick. In a moment of desperation, I realize I'm no longer driving this train.

The bewitched widower has fallen under Satan's spell and is a second away from releasing the hands of Tenkiller and Luanne.

I am still under the devil's power, unable to act, to move, to scream. I can't do shit except for watching this bitch derail. Grumann releases his hands and steps toward the apparition, breaking the spiritual protection of our circle.

The invisible barrier that separated us from Satan, as well as the holy light flowing from above, dissipate and die a harsh death.

Grumann reaches out to his wife.

She opens her arms to embrace him.

When they touch, an aura of evil pulses over the couple, and a deafening explosion spawns utter chaos. The violent concussion hammers the team backward as flames shoot upward. The stench of sulfur and burning flesh violate our lungs.

What had once been a living, breathing man is now a pile of ashes. Standing in the center of the glowing embers is Satan. The Master of Deceit.

The rejuvenated ruler of Hell.

I fear he will be the last thing we see before our painful death.

59

FUR, FURY, AND FANGS

"JACQUI? LUANNE?" THE SMOKE SLOWLY clears, and I choke on the noxious fumes of incinerated human remains. My two female friends brush themselves off, and the three of us cross the media room to Tenkiller and Rambo.

I check my watch, and the breath catches in my throat. Time is slipping away to release the two connected worlds. But I have more pressing issues as Satan takes a step toward us. Tenkiller hears the motion and gallantly moves to block the devil's approach.

"Stop!" The angel puts his hand out.

"Who's going to make me?" The devil crosses his arms and sneers. "Some washed out addict? A has been angel? A drunk, blind refugee from life who sleeps in a coffin and relies on an ill-tempered mutt to lead him to his next piece of ass?"

Tenkiller hangs his head and rubs the beginning tears from his sightless eyes.

"Oh, did I hurt your little feelings?" Satan holds his leathery hand out, and a pint of gin materializes. With a deft twist, he opens the bottle. "I know you can't see what I'm holding, but you can smell it."

He passes the liquor under Ten's nose.

My hand is on the angel's shoulder as I peer around his

body. Fear rips through my gut when I see the longing upon his countenance. Tenkiller inhales the fumes, and the obvious enjoyment lights up his face.

I shake him hard. "Fight it. Don't give in."

The devil puts the bottle against Tenkiller's lips. "When life gets hard, you get soft and weak. So, take a drink, and this will all go away."

Ten takes a mouthful, and my heart hits rock bottom.

Satan smirks. "That's a good boy."

The angel leans back then jerks forward and spits the gin in the devil's face.

Ten's sightless eyes open wide. "I. Will. Not. Do. This!"

"You piece of shit, you will because you can't live with your past. Because you let ten people die. And because you are weak and a drunk—a fallen angel who's lost his wings." Satan wipes the liquor from his face. "How many times will you continue to fail before you realize Heaven would be better off without your sorry ass?

"My way is easy, so drink the gin. Let it ease your mind and free your soul. Then drift off into the darkness. A place of no more troubles. No more guilt. And no more pain."

I press my hand against Tenkiller's torso. Trembling radiates through his core, and I see his intense longing as he reaches for the liquor. His fingers quiver, and his act of defiance a minute ago must have been pure bravado.

I fist both hands and shake them. "Don't do it!"

The fallen angel brings the bottle to his lips, closes his eyes, then grins at the devil before he throws the gin on the floor. The glass shatters, and Tenkiller screams, "Go rot in Hell!"

Satan raises to his full height and backhands Ten.

Unable to defend himself, the blind angel reels from the blow. But, a look of righteous anger creases his face.

The devil releases his rage with a devastating punch to Ten's stomach. Then assaults his unprotected face with vicious jabs, once, twice, three times. Satan shrieks with glee when he kicks the angel in the balls.

Ten falls to the floor, grips his groin, and curls into a fetal position. Satan puts his heel on Ten's head and pushes down. "You should have taken the gin. It's the easy way out for a loser like you."

At that moment, a streak of fur, fury, and fangs charges from Tenkiller's side and attacks Lucifer's calf, burying sharp incisors deep into his leathery flesh.

The tiny dog, maddened with rage, fights to protect its master, fights against insurmountable odds, fights with feral savagery until the devil shakes him loose and brutally kicks him in the side.

Rambo is thrown across the floor and cries out repeatedly. His tiny body convulses, twists, and shudders before silence reclaims the room.

I drop to Ten's side and comfort him. The heart-breaking horror and savagery infuriate Tenkiller who moans as he rises from the floor. Blood streams from his nose, his left eye is purple and swollen shut, and both lips need sutures. But he ignores his injuries and extends his hand to help me up. "The three of you surround me, hold tight, and concentrate on your psychic powers."

We move closer toward the angel, and I sense the courage of an unexpected hero as he drapes his arms around us.

"This may get ugly, so whatever happens, don't let go!"

A glance at my watch, and I bite my lower lip. Seven minutes until the two worlds explode. Fifteen more before my body on Earth dies. I look over at Rambo, and my gut tightens with anger. I swear upon all that is holy that I will kick Satan's ass. And I will do it in the next five minutes.

After a deep breath, I ask God for guidance, then concentrate on my psychic power.

60

IN GOD WE TRUST

STANDING IN THE CENTER OF the media room, the portal connecting Earth with this alternate planet is on our left, while to the right are the twelve luxury media room recliners. Tenkiller motions the other two Sisters of the Triumvirate and me closer as he repeats the Lord's Prayer. A cone of protection now encircles us while Satan cusses our effort to coalesce the three sisters' powers and connect with God.

The devil's lips move, and he shakes a leathery fist at us. But we are effectively insulated from him by a transparent dome that shimmers with life. I reach out to touch it and am pleasantly shocked by its spiritual current—a force that transmits divine love with the feeling of unconditional acceptance. It's as if I have slumbered all my life, awakened, and found my true home.

I look up at Tenkiller's eyes and recoil. Instead of an iris and pupil dominated by a circular blast of Arctic white and encircled by a thin ring of penetrating blue, both eyes color are now a normal brown and black.

A shudder passes through his body, and the feeling of divine love escalates. The skin on my neck prickles when I feel the back of his pink woman's stretch top expand beneath my fingers. Momentarily, it rips apart.

Enriched by this aura of goodness, love, and spirituality, Tenkiller's wings emerge from the hump between his shoulders and continue to grow. Rapidly. Extending into a mighty wingspread of ten feet each covered with pure white plumage. The forward edge, or patagium, is seven feet long and leads to the primary feathers at the end of the wings. Underneath are the secondary feathers, all pristine as the driven snow.

I realize from this action that we are not forgotten because from a mighty God comes mighty things. I gape at the angel's massive spread, now extended shoulder height to the left and right. And my gut says it's our turn to kick Satan's ass.

The emergence of Ten's wings enrages the devil, who fists his leathery hands and beats upon the clear cone that separates us. A primal scream releases a cloud of black particles from his mouth. Darkness that grows in intensity and volume until Satan's body dissipates and transforms into a dark, bitter cloud which rotates around our clear barrier.

My fear spikes as the howl of lost souls hidden within the vile cover of blackness rises. Jacqui and Luanne's faces twist with shock and terror.

The obsidian cloud begins to slow its rotation until it stops, then reverses its direction. The terrible screams embedded within the darkness earlier now reveal their source in a whirlwind that whips pale bodies around the cone. White, bloodless corpses with unseeing eyes and death's head grins. Human remains are thrown, smashed, and beaten against our fragile barrier until I fear it will rupture.

I cover my head and scream.

But the hideous onslaught continues. And after several minutes, it diminishes in intensity until the black cloud halts.

I take a quick breath as the bloodless ghouls retreat from view, summoned back to whatever pit they emerged from.

But Satan is not finished because the stilled black cloud pulls back and reforms above us into a pulsing mass of darkness that pounds against the top of our protective dome—smashing over and over until tiny cracks run through the barrier. My sense of safety is in disarray, like a crazy quilt of schizophrenic stitches.

I look upward and regret it immediately. The hideous darkness begins to ooze through a dozen minute fissures in the dome, extending itself until it reaches about sixteen inches. Then, it expands and forms dismembered forearms with intact hands and fingers. Twelve dark arms begin to crawl down the inside of the dome toward us, creeping closer with horrifying intent.

One severed limb releases itself and drops to our left, only to dissolve into a hissing pool of acid that disintegrates the concrete below.

Tenkiller can see the threat and hear the snap and pop beside him. "Get underneath!"

Jacqui, Luanne, and I burrow against Ten's torso as his beautiful wings fold over our heads in a protective embrace, covering us with the soft down of angel's feathers, keeping us safe from the acidic onslaught above.

Protected beneath this heavenly awning, I feel the impact as the dark arms from above fall onto Ten's wings. They release their acidic content which eats through his unprotected flesh and feathers, crippling him with excruciating pain.

Ten gasps for air, then clenches his teeth. "Archer, if we're going to get spiritual help, it's gotta be quick. His wings shudder around us. "I can't hold on much longer."

I grip Luanne's hand, then Jacqui's. "All right girls, concentrate and focus on our psychic powers."

The angel screams a long, piercing note that rips my soul, ignites my anger, and fuels my resolve. I focus upon my paranormal gifts, embrace my psychic birthright, thrust my heart and soul into connecting with the other two Sisters of the Triumvirate.

Jacqui and Luanne grip my hands as the floor shakes. Tenkiller shrieks again, this time from mortal injury. His wings shake from the acid eating through flesh, bone, and feathers.

"I'm sorry, Archer," Tenkiller cries. "I failed, just like before. I killed the ten people under my care. Now, I can't save the three of you."

The wings protecting Jacqui, Luanne, and I are moments away from dissipating and allowing acid to flush over us. We still haven't connected our psychic powers yet. And then it hits me. We are focusing on the wrong thing. The three sisters are close to God. But as an angel, Tenkiller is closer!

I shake my two friend's shoulders. "Concentrate on Tenkiller and establish a spiritual link to embellish his divine connection."

The three of us concentrate, focus, and feel the transition, a spiritual bond that imbues us with the presence of sacredness. A divine connection that flares and blinds our physical eyes with its radiance. On a soul level, it presents us with a gift. A gift to the righteous searchers. A gift called the pathway to God.

Jacqui, Luanne, Tenkiller, and I absorb the spiritual light from the presence of the Almighty. All around us is a living aura of divinity. And within this domain, darkness cannot survive.

Our protective dome is gone. The stygian cloud that was Satan, gone also. And the dismembered forearms. They are gone, too.

Tenkiller slowly unfolds his wings.

The Three Sisters of the Triumvirate step back, gasping at the miracles before us. Ten's wings are restored to their spiritual glory, completely healed and untouched. And the second miracle barks and jumps at his master's leg. Rambo is alive!

With a cry of jubilation, my friends hug each other and bask in our accomplishment until I glance at my watch.

"Oh, shit!" It's all I can say because we have less than two minutes before Earth and this alternate world explode. I reach into my pocket for the pentagon-shaped key, then gasp in horror.

It's freakin' gone!

THE NEWLY RISEN

I IMMEDIATELY TAKE COMMAND OF the situation in the devil's media room. "Jacqui, Luanne, check under the twelve recliners for the portal key. "Tenkiller, go back and search the floor and wall's baseboards."

This screw-up shouldn't be happening. Not now and so close to two planetary explosions. One and one-half minutes left, and I'm about to throw my hands up and scream. But losing control won't keep us alive.

Jacqui and Luanne hurriedly check beneath the recliners as well as under the seat cushions. Without wasting a second, they scan the linoleum behind the chairs in addition to the floor opposite of Ten.

Tenkiller turns his palm's up. "It's not here, Archer."

By the look on his face, he is fried, frayed, and filleted.

"We can't find it either," Jacqui admits defeat as she and Luanne step back to me. Their cheeks are flushed, eyes brimming with tears.

At that moment, with one minute left, Rambo barks and howls while jumping against the back of Ten's wings.

The room goes silent, and I remember the same behavior when the dog needed to pee earlier. "Rambo's giving us a clue. Tenkiller spread your wings and flutter them. Hard."

I quickly move away as he opens his wingspan. He flaps once, twice, and on the third try, the portal key dislodges from the secondary feathers on the underside of his wings.

"It must have lodged there when I was bumped around from the falling limbs." I grab the key from the floor and look at my watch. Forty-five seconds left before our time flatlines. "Jacqui, Luanne, cross over the portal to Earth. Now!"

The two girls step across and wait for me on the other side.

I stand opposite them in a world where my alternate parents, their daughter, and her boyfriend didn't want me. And would have murdered me if they'd had their way. My dream was to regain the love I'd lost after I had killed my birth parents. But this fairytale took a detour to the dead zone. And the only way out is for me to leave. Leave the alternate Archer's body and reclaim my life on Earth.

With the last action I require of my doppelganger, she acquiesces and slips the pentagonal key in the portal receptacle above.

And now it's time to put plan B in motion. "Luanne, plant the memories."

Less than twenty seconds remain before the two worlds explode. My astral spirit pulls away from the alternate Archer, and I crawl through the closing portal just in time to reconnect with my real body in the hospital room on Earth.

As my astral spirit eases back into my physical shell, an electric surge fires through my reclaimed body, rejuvenating my system, charging my mental prowess. Lying on my side, I open my eyes to see Jacqui and Luanne standing in front of me while holding my hand.

"Congo rats, Archer, you averted the planetary meltdown!" Jacqui winks at me.

My mouth is desert dry, and I nod at the water pitcher. Luanne pours me a glass, adds a straw, and places it against my lips.

I noisily suck until I get my fill, then pull away.

I try to regain control of my dormant muscles and clumsily flip from my side to my back, then kick the bed sheet down below my stomach where I notice a bulge. An unexpected bulge. A where the hell did this come from baby bulge.

"What the devil?" I'm confused, confounded, and just copped a ride on the crazy train.

Both girls gasp. And Luanne points. "Archer… you are *so* pregnant!" Her eyes open wide.

"This might explain things, Arch." Jacqui hands me an envelope lying on the bedside table with block letters.

WHEN YOU AWAKE.

My hands shake as I open it. My heart rate shifts into hyperdrive, and even though it's warm inside, I shiver. Clearing my throat first, I read out loud, "Had a feeling you'd come back to your body, so let me be the first to say congratulations because we're going to be parents."

I try to sit up, but my muscles have atrophied after six months of disuse, and I gratefully accept Luanne's assistance. I've been sexually violated and absent from my body for half a year. And I wonder if the baby would be healthy with my astral spirit gone for so long. So, I scramble for some explanation as to how this happened. And the obvious question of who is the father?

The last time I had sex was with Slash, my Earthbound boyfriend, about six months ago and had my period shortly after. Slash can't be the father. So, who is?

I take a closer look at the hand-printed letter, searching for a name or clue toward its author.

Nothing. Nada.

Zero. Zip.

That is until I find a small piece of paper taped inside the envelope with a local seven-digit phone number.

"Luanne, call this for me." I hand her the slip and accept the handset as she dials.

I slowly count seven rings before someone answers.

"This must be Archer."

The voice is strained but familiar. I can't place him. Not yet.

"I take it sleeping beauty has awakened."

I'm not in the mood for games, so I level with the mystery man. "Cut to the punchline. Who the hell are you?"

"Is this any way to talk to the father of your child?"

"Put a name to the voice. Who. Are. You?"

The line goes silent. Silence so deep I can hear faint voices from a television in the background. Then, a sigh.

"Archer, I will be there when you go into labor. I will be there when you deliver our baby. And I will be there to watch you die after our young child drives a knife into your heart. I am part of your past, all your present, and the few years that remain of your future. I will be the primary force behind your every conscious thought. From this point on, until you die, you will think of me.

"For I am your worst fear.

"A demon come to life.

"The Frankenstein of your nightmares.

"But you can call me, Le Cadavre."

My heart stops beating for a moment. I grip the phone so hard my hand shakes. "This can't be true. I killed you in an alternate world over six months ago."

"Let's say I've risen from the dead, Archer, and am ready to embrace the challenge of fatherhood."

A mind-numbing fog settles upon me as I look at my belly. Six months ago I was screwed, blued, and tattooed—an unwilling part of the process that has left me pregnant, perturbed, and pretty pissed off.

But I'll not take this lying down. "Neither you *nor* my unborn child will kill me. Once I get out of here, you should watch your back because I'm coming for *you.*"

"I see you still have piss and vinegar in your veins." The caller chuckles. *"If it's a girl, we should name her Archer."*

Evil as old as antiquity rips across the center of my soul. A crippling pain shoots through my head. My vision dims. And his last words have injected a terminal frost to the remainder my heart.

What the hell have I gotten into?

EPILOGUE: IT'S A WRAP

KNOCKED UP AND UNWED, ARCHER was left in a pretty pickle, but at least she's alive. So, what happened to the rest of our characters? Well, Luanne's special psychic gift was being able to plant a memory in someone's mind. A recollection that was so vivid, so real, it felt like the truth. And that's exactly what Archer asked her to do just before the portal closed. The thirteen escaped felons received implanted memories in which they worked as correctional officers at the alternate world's Amarillo maximum security unit. Morgan Fairview III also "remembered" being the Chief Financial Officer at the same facility. Luanne further suggested that the CFO come clean about Jason Blaine's hidden millions and donate the funds to a local hospice.

When the felons showed up for work the next morning at the prison, the correctional officers recognized the escapees and handled their apprehension diligently and professionally. Even though Morgan Fairview had served his sentence, he insisted on divulging the paper trail to Jason Blaine's illicit resources.

Luanne and Jacqui were tempted by the devil, who insisted he could bring back their dead loved ones. But both women made peace with their losses and recognized God's natural order of life and death.

Charity, the hooker, is still walking Sixth Street in Amarillo, Texas. She is a little bit older, somewhat wiser, and has a special place in her heart for Tenkiller.

The force behind Tenkiller, Colonel Landers, the man who kept believing that everyone deserved a second chance, was promoted to be the guardian angel of the president and his administration. After a short trip to the Bahamas and a few stiff drinks, the go-to guy was fortified enough to begin his new heavenly duties.

Lee Kale, the prison mailman, quit his job at the maximum security unit, sold his house in Amarillo, and purchased a home in Denver, Colorado, where he, his young child, and his new girlfriend, Hope, the psychic empath, live

When Hope finally touched Lee Kale, she had no illness to absorb. Because of Hope's unique gift, Lee declined the unneeded expense of health insurance for him and his son.

Dr. Ron Smith, the ER facility owner, donated his collection of purloined ladies' shoes to a local women's shelter. It is a place where Prada is distributed alongside Jimmy Choo, thereby providing the most stylish and fashionable footwear to the homeless women in Amarillo.

And let's not forget the cantankerous Rambo. Since the dog's owner, Tenkiller, can now see, his services are no longer required. So, the four-pound canine spends his days sunning in a spacious yard, chasing the neighbor's cats, and intimidating the mailman regularly.

The last time we had seen Satan was when he dissolved into a black cloud of evil that encircled Ten's protective dome. After Archer and her team connected with a higher power, the cloud disappeared because evil cannot bear the presence of God. However, when Satan regained his physical shape, there was a slight glitch. The butt of one of the ghouls that circled the dome earlier was present during the reformation and accidentally replaced the devil's face.

Satan now had two opposing butt cheeks extending from the forehead to the bottom jaw. With a vertical crack between the two.

And the devil's new mouth was as puckered as if he'd bitten into a lemon. Then, adding excess to egregious injury, one of Satan's eyes tracked off to the left, which confused those talking with the devil because no one could figure out which eye to look at.

Even though Satan returned to his throne, his street creds were in tatters, and his sycophantic followers dubbed him ass face behind his back. Under his reign, the term ass kisser took on a new meaning.

Last, but not least, Tenkiller gave up his blood splashed, graffiti-splattered coffin in the failed Amarillo spiritual ministry for some nicer digs in Taos, New Mexico. Specifically, a one-hundred-year-old adobe art studio with magnificent light from a western exposure. His three students were called to him by a series of visions, spiritual manifestations, and dreams. Individually, each artist was refreshingly humble and had a unique style, which made Tenkiller's job so much easier. His goal was to guide each student in the expression of his or her soul and to reach and surpass the genius of the Old Masters.

The visual subject would be God's angels, starting with His fierce and holy warriors, then capturing the warmth and love of humanity's guardians, as well as the innocence and divinity of the Cherubs. Tenkiller would be responsible for the spiritual Renaissance of angelic art. Art that will capture the breath of its viewer, unlock the heart, and summon an overpowering feeling of brotherhood and love.

Such were the keys given to Tenkiller—a fallen angel who never stopped loving God. And a God who never stopped loving him.

MICHAEL DAVID graduated with honors from West Texas A&M in 1988, earning a BBA in Finance. For the next two years, he worked as an assistant examiner for the FDIC during the banking crisis of the late 80's. By then, though, Michael had decided to heed the call to become a writer and quit his job in 1990. Then found a position in Amarillo, Texas, working with people with disabilities, and began writing.

He is the author of six novels and two screenplays, and is currently writing the third and fourth installments of The Psionic Sequence series.

Michael is now retired, and resides in Amarillo, Texas.

MICHAELDAVIDAUTHOR.COM